D0052451

BAPTISM OF FIRE

Eight weeks of special training had failed to prepare him for the silent insanity of space warfare. Disintegration and silent death, the pinpoints of distant light that were laser beams locked on to his ship, the stormy marriage of anti-particles, the grotesque beauty of short-lived spherical explosions— bolts of launched lightning, blue and white, igniting the proper combination of gases...

Rick Hunter fired the VT's thrusters as two Battlepods closed in on him from above— the relative above at any rate, for there was no actual up or down out here, no real way to gauge acceleration except by the constant force that kept him pinned to the back of his seat or pushed him forward when the retros were kicked in, no way to judge velocity except in relation to other Veritech fighters or the SDF-1 itself. Just that unvarying starfield, those cool and remote fires that were the backdrop of war.

The ROBOTECH™ Series
Published by Ballantine Books:

ROBOTECH™ #2:

BATTLE CRY

Jack McKinney

A Del Rey Book

BALLANTINE BOOKS • NEW YORK

A Del Rey Book
Published by Ballantine Books

Copyright © 1987 by Harmony Gold U.S.A., Inc. and Tatsunoko Production Co., Ltd.

All rights reserved under International and Pan-American Copyright Conventions. Published in the United States of America by Ballantine Books, a division of Random House, Inc., New York, and simultaneously in Canada by Random House of Canada Limited, Toronto.

Library of Congress Catalog Card Number: 86-91633

ISBN 0-345-34134-1

Printed in Canada

First Edition: March 1987

Cover art by David Schleinkofer

FOR CARMEN, CARLOS, AND DIMITRI
MAMARONECK'S ROBOTECH DEFENSE FORCE

CHAPTER
ONE

If there was any one thing that typified the initial stages of the First Robotech War, it was the unspoken interplay that developed between Captain Henry Gloval and the Zentraedi commander, Breetai. In effect, both men had been created for warfare—Gloval by the Soviet GRU, and Breetai, of course, by the Robotech Masters. When one examines the early ship's log entries of the two commanders, it is evident that each man spent a good deal of time trying to analyze the personality of his opponent by way of the strategies each employed. Breetai was perhaps at an advantage here, having at his disposal volumes of Zentraedi documents devoted to legends regarding the origin of Micronian societies. But it must be pointed out that Breetai was severely limited by his prior conditioning in his attempts to interpret these: even Exedore, who had been bred to serve as transcultural adviser, would fail him on this front. Gloval, on the other hand, with little knowledge of his ship and even less of his opponent, had the combined strengths of a loyal and intelligent crew to draw upon and the instincts of one who had learned to function best in situations where disinformation and speculation were the norm. One could point to many examples of this, but perhaps none is so representative of the group mind at work inboard the SDF-1 than the Battle at Saturn's Rings.

"Genesis," *History of the First Robotech War,* Vol. XVII

ZOR'S SHIP, THE SDF-1, MOVED THROUGH DEEP space like some creature loosed from an ancient sea fable. The structural transformation the fortress had undergone at the hands of its new commanders had rendered it monsterlike—an appearance reinforced by those oceangoing vessels grafted on to it like arms and the main gun towers that rose now from the body like twin heads, horned and threatening.

What would the Robotech Masters make of this new design? Breetai asked himself. Even prior to the transformation, Zor's ship was vastly different from his own —indeed, different from any vessel of the Zentraedi fleet. Protoculture factory that it was, it had always lacked the amorphous *organic* feel Breetai preferred. But then, it had not been designed as a warship. Until now.

The Zentraedi commander was on the bridge of his vessel, where an image of the SDF-1 played across the silent field of a projecbeam. Breetai's massive arms were folded across the brown tunic of his uniform, and the monocular enhancer set in the plate that covered half his face was trained on the free-floating screen.

Long-range scopes had captured this image of the ship for his inspection and analysis. But what those same scopes and scanners failed to reveal was the makeup of the creatures who possessed it.

The bridge was an observation bubble overlooking the astrogational center of the flagship, a vast gallery of screens, projecbeam fields, and holo-schematics that gave Breetai access to information gathered by any cruiser or destroyer in his command. He could communicate with any of his many officers or any of the numerous Cyclops recon ships. But none of these could furnish him with the data he now desired—some explanation of Micronian behavior. For that, Breetai counted on Exedore, his dwarfish adviser, who at the moment seemed equally at a loss.

"Commander," the misshapen man was saying, "I have analysed this most recent strategy from every possible angle, and I *still* cannot understand why they found it necessary to change to this format. A structural modification of this nature will most assuredly diminish, possibly even negate, the effectiveness of the ship's gravity control centers."

"And their weapons?"

"Fully operational. Unless they are diverting energy to one of the shield systems."

Breetai wondered whether he was being overly cautious. It was true that he had been caught off guard by the Micronians' unpredictable tactics but unlikely that he had underestimated their capabilities. That they had chosen to execute an intraatmospheric spacefold, heedless of the effects of their island population center, was somewhat disturbing, as was their most recent use of the powerful main gun of the SDF-l. But these were surely acts of desperation, those of an enemy running scared, not one in full possession of the situation.

In any straightforward military exercise, this unpredictability would have posed no threat. It had been Breetai's experience that superior firepower invariably won out over desperate acts or clever tactics. And there were few in the known universe who could rival the Zentraedi in firepower. But this operation called for a certain finesse. The Micronians would ultimately be defeated; of this he was certain. Defeat, however, was of secondary importance. His prime directive was to recapture Zor's ship undamaged, and given the Micronian penchant for self-destruction, a successful outcome could not be guaranteed.

With this in mind Breetai had adopted a policy of watchful waiting. For more than two months by Micronian reckoning, the Zentraedi fleet had followed the SDF-1 without launching an attack. During that time, he and Exedore had monitored the ship's movements and audiovisual transmissions; they had analyzed the changes and modifications Zor's ship had undergone; they had screened trans-vids of their initial confrontations with the enemy. And most important, they had studied the Zentraedi legends regarding Micronian societies. There were warnings in those legends—warnings Breetai had chosen to ignore.

The SDF-1 was approaching an outer planet of this yellow-star system, a ringed world, large and gaseous, with numerous small moons. A secondary screen on the flagship bridge showed it to be the system's sixth planet. Exedore, who had already made great progress in deciphering the Micronian language, had its name: Saturn.

"My lord, I suspect that the spacefold generators aboard Zor's ship may have been damaged during the hyperspace jump from Earth to the outer planets. My belief is that the Micronians will attempt to use the gravity of this planet to sling themselves toward their homeworld."

"Interesting," Breetai replied.

"Furthermore, they will probably activate ECM as they near the planetary rings. It may become difficult for us to lock in on their course."

"It is certainly the logical choice, Exedore. And that is precisely what concerns me. They have yet to demonstrate any knowledge of logic."

"Your decision, my lord?"

"They have more than an escape plan in mind. The firepower of the main gun has given them confidence in their ability to engage us." Breetai stroked his chin as he watched the screen. "I'll let them attempt their clever little plan, if only to gain a clearer understanding of their tactics. I'm curious to see if they are in full possession of the power that ship holds."

Henry Gloval, formerly of the supercarriers *Kenosha* and *Prometheus* and now captain of the super dimensional fortress, the SDF-1, was a practical man of few words and even fewer expectations. When it came to asking himself how he had ended up in command of an alien spaceship, 1,500,000,000 kilometers from home base and carrying almost 60,000 civilians in its belly, he refused to let the question surface more than twice a day.

And yet here was the planet Saturn filling the forward bays of the SDF-1's bridge, and here was Henry Gloval in the command chair treating it like just one more Pacific current he'd have to navigate. Well, not quite: No one he'd encountered during his long career as a naval officer had ever used an ocean current the way he planned to use Saturn's gravitational fields.

The SDF-1; spacefold generators, which two months ago had allowed the ship to travel through hyperspace from Earth to Pluto in a matter of minutes, had vanished. Perhaps "allowed" was the wrong word, since Gloval had had his sights on the moon at the time. But no matter—the disappearance remained a mystery for Dr. Lang and his Robotechs to unravel; it had fallen on Gloval's shoulders to figure a way back home without the generators.

Even by the year 2010 the book on interplanetary travel was far from complete; in fact, Lang, Gloval, and a few others were still writing it. Each situation faced was a new one, each new maneuver potentially the last. There had been any number of unmanned outer-planet probes, and of course the Armor Series orbital stations and the lunar and Martian bases, but travel beyond the asteroid belt had never been undertaken by a human crew. Who was to say how it might have been if the Global Civil War hadn't put an end to the human experiment in space? But that was the way the cards had been dealt, and in truth, humankind had the SDF-1 to thank for getting things started again, even if the ship was now more weapon than spacecraft. All this, however, would be for the historians to figure out. Gloval had more pressing concerns.

Relatively speaking, the Earth was on the far side of the sun. The fortress's reflex engines would get them home, but not quickly, and even then they were going to need a healthy send-off from Saturn. Engineering's plan was for the ship to orbit the planet and make use of centrifugal force to sling her on her way. It was not an entirely untested plan but a dangerous one nonetheless. And there was one more factor Gloval had to figure into the calculations: the enemy.

Unseen in full force, unnamed, unknown. Save that they were thought to be sixty-foot-tall humanoids of seemingly limitless supply. They had appeared in Earth-space a little more than two months ago and declared war on the planet. There was no way of knowing what fate had befallen Earth after the SDF-1's hyperspace jump, but some of the enemy fleet—or, for all Gloval knew, a splinter group—had pursued the ship clear across the solar system to press the attack. The SDF-1's main gun had saved them once, but firing it had required a modular transformation which had not only wreaked havoc with many of the ship's secondary systems but had nearly destroyed the city that had grown up within it.

For two months now the enemy had left the ship

alone. They allowed themselves to be picked up by radar and scanners but were careful not to reveal the size of their fleet. Sometimes it appeared that Battlepods made up the bulk of their offensive strength—those oddly shaped, one-pilot mecha the VT teams called "headless ostriches." At other times there was evidence of scout ships and recon vessels, cruisers and destroyers. But if the enemy's numbers were a source for speculation, their motives seemed to be clear: They had come for their ship, the SDF-1.

Gloval was not about to let them have it without a fight. Perhaps if they'd come calling and *asked* for the ship, something could have been arranged. But that, too, was history.

There was only one way to guarantee a safe return to Earth: They had to either shake the enemy from their tail or destroy them. Gloval had been leaning toward the former approach until Dr. Lang had surprised him with the latest of his daily discoveries.

Lang was Gloval's interface with the SDF-1; more than anyone else onboard, the German scientist had re-tuned his thinking to that of the technicians who had originally built the ship. He had accomplished on a grand scale what the Veritech fighter pilots were expected to do on each mission: meld their minds to the mecha con-trols. There was suspicion among the crew that Lang had plugged himself into one of the SDF-1's stock computers and taken some sort of mind boost which had put him in touch with the ship's builders, leaving him a stranger to those who hadn't. Gloval often felt like he was dealing with an alien entity when speaking to Lang—he couldn't bring himself to make contact with those marblelike eyes. It was as if the passionate side of the man's nature had been drained away and replaced with some of the strange fluids that coursed through many of the ship's living systems. You didn't exchange pleasantries with a man like Lang; you went directly to the point and linked memory banks with him. So when Lang told him that it might be possible to create a protective envelope for the SDF-1, Gloval merely asked how long it would take to develop.

The two men met in the chamber that until recently had housed the spacefold generators. Lang wanted Gloval to see for himself the free-floating mesmerizing energy that had spontaneously appeared there with the disappearance of the generators. Later they moved to Lang's quarters, the only section of the unreconstructed fortress sized to human proportions. There the scientist explained that the energy had something to do with a local distortion in the spacetime continuum. Gloval couldn't follow all the details of the theories involved, but he stayed with it long enough to understand that this same energy could be utilized in the fabrication of a shield system for the SDF-1.

Since his conversation with Dr. Lang, Gloval had become preoccupied with the idea of taking the enemy by surprise with an offensive maneuver. With the main guns now operational and the potential of a protective barrier, Gloval and the SDF-1 would be able to secure an unobstructed route back to Earth. And Saturn, with its many moons and rings, was ideally suited to such a purpose.

Rick Hunter, Veritech cadet, admired his reflection in the shop windows along Macross City's main street. He stopped once or twice to straighten the pleats in his trousers, adjust the belt that cinched his colorful jacket, or give his long black hair just the right look of stylish disarray. It was his first day of leave after eight weeks of rigorous training, and he had never felt better. Or looked better, to judge from the attention he was getting from passersby, especially the young women of the transplanted city.

Rick was always reasonably fit—years of stunt flying had necessitated that—but the drill sergeants had turned his thin frame wiry and tough. "Nothing extraneous, in mind or body." Rick had adopted their motto as his own. He had even learned a few new flying tricks (and taught the instructors a few himself). Planes had been his life for nineteen years, and even the weightlessness of deep space felt like his element. He wasn't as comfortable with weapons, though, and the idea of killing a living creature was still as alien to him as it had been two months ago. But Roy Fokker, Rick's "older brother," was helping him through this rough period. Roy had talked about his own early misgivings, about how you had to think of the Battlepods as mecha, about how *real* the enemy threat was to all of them inboard the SDF-1. "'The price of liberty is eternal vigilance'," Roy said, quoting an American president. "There's no more flying for fun. This time you'll be flying for your home and the safety of your loved ones." Of course Roy had been through the Global Civil War; he had experience in death and destruction. He'd even come through it a decorated soldier. Although why anyone would have sought that out remained a mystery to Rick. Roy had left Pop Hunter's flying circus for that circus of global madness, and it wasn't something Rick liked to think about. Besides, as true as it might be that the war was right outside any hatch of the ship, it was surely a long way off for a cadet whose battle experience thus far had been purely accidental.

Rick was strolling down Macross Boulevard at a leisurely pace; he still had a few minutes to kill before meeting Minmei at the market. The city had managed to completely rebuild what the modular transformation had left in ruins. Taking into account the SDF-1's ability to mechamorphose, the revised city plan relied on a vertical axis of orientation. The attempt to recreate the horizontal openness of Macross Island was abandoned. The new city rose in three tiers toward the ceiling of the massive hold. Ornate bridges spanned structural troughs; environmental control units and the vast recycling system had been integrated into the high-tech design of the buildings; EVE engineers—specialists in enhanced video emulation—were experimenting with sky and horizon effects; hydroponics had supplied trees and shrubs; and a monorail was under construction. The city planners had also worked out many of the problems that had plagued the city early on. Shelters and yellow and black safety areas were well marked in the event of modular transformation. Each resident now had a bed to sleep in, a job to perform. Food and water rationing was accepted as part of the routine. The system of waivers, ration coupons, and military scrip had proved manageable. Most people had navigated the psychological crossings successfully. There would soon be a television station, and a lottery was in the works. In general the city was not unlike a turn-of-the-century shopping mall, except in size and population. Remarkably, the residents of Macross had made the adjustment—they were a special lot from the start—and the general feeling there was a cross between that found in an experimental prototype community and that found in any of the wartime cities of the last era.

Nearing the market now, Rick began to focus his thoughts on Minmei and how the day as he imagined it would unfold. She would be knocked out by the sight of him in uniform; she wouldn't be able to keep her hands off him; he would suggest the park, and she would eagerly agree—

"Rick!"

Minmei was running toward him, a full shopping bag cradled in one arm, her free hand waving like mad. She was wearing a tight sleeveless sweater over a white blouse, and a skirt that revealed too much. Her hair was down, lustrous even in the city's artificial light; her blue eyes were bright, fixed on his as she kissed him once and stepped back to give him the once-over.

Inside the cool and and crisp cadet Rick was projecting, his heart was running wild. She was already talking a blue streak, filling him in on her eight weeks, asking questions about "spacic training," complimenting him, the uniform, the Defense Force, the mayor, and everyone else connected with the war effort. Rick, however, was so drawn to her beauty that he scarcely heard the news or compliments; he was suddenly quiet and worried. Minmei drew stares from everyone they passed, and she appeared to know half of Macross personally. What had she been doing these past eight weeks—introducing herself on street corners? And what was all this about singing lessons, dance lessons, and an upcoming beauty pageant? Rick wanted to tell her about the hardships of training, the new friends he'd made, his unvoiced fears; he wanted to hold her and tell her how much he had missed her, tell her how their two-week ordeal together had been one of the most precious times in his life. But she wasn't letting him get a word in.

A short distance down the block, Minmei stopped in midsentence and dragged Rick over to one of the storefronts. In the window was a salmon-colored belted dress that had suddenly become the most important thing in the world to her.

"Come on, Rick, just for a minute, okay?"

"Minmei," he resisted, "I'm not going to spend my leave shopping."

"I promise I'll only be a second."

"It always starts out that way and, and . . ."

Minmei already had her hand on the doorknob. "Just what else did you have in mind for today, Rick?"

She disappeared into the woman's shop, leaving him standing on the sidewalk, feeling somehow guilty for even *thinking* about going to the park.

By the time he entered, Minmei had the hangered dress draped over one arm and was going through the racks, pulling out belts, blouses, patterned stockings, skirts, sweaters, and lingerie. Rick checked his watch and calculated that he'd be AWOL long before she finished trying everything on. She had entered the dressing room and was throwing the curtain closed.

"And no peeking, Rick," she called out.

Fortunately there were no other customers in the store at the time, but the saleswoman standing silently behind Rick had found Minmei's warning just about the funniest thing she had heard all week. Her squeal of delight took Rick completely by surprise. He thought an early-warning signal had just gone off—and in the middle of squatting down for cover, he managed to lose some of the items from the top of the shopping bag. In stooping over to recover these, he tipped the bag, spilling half the contents across the floor.

The woman was laughing like a maniac now, the door buzzer was signaling the entry of three additional shoppers, and Minmei was peeking over the top of the dressing room curtain asking what had happened. Rick, meanwhile, was down on his hands and knees crawling under tables in search of the goods—bottles of shampoo, creme rinse, body lotion, baby oil, lipsticks, and sundry makeup containers—all of which had become covered in some sort of slippery wash from a container of liquid face soap that had partially opened. Each time Rick grabbed hold of one of the items, it would jump from his hand like a wet fish. But he soon got the hang of it and had almost everything rebagged in a short time. Only one thing left to retrieve: a tube of tricolored toothpaste just out of reach, bathing in a puddle of the face soap. Rick gave it a shot, stretching out and making a grab for it. Sure enough, the tube propelled itself and ended up under another table.

It was time to get serious. Rick set the bag aside and crawled off stealthily after his prey, as though the tube had taken on a will of its own and was on the verge of scurrying off, like some of Macross City's robo-dispenser units. He squinted, held the tube in his gaze, and when he was near enough, pounced.

The tube seemed to scream in his hands and immediately worked itself into a vertical launch. But Rick had prepared himself for this; he lifted his head, eyes fixed on the tube's ascent.

The one thing he hadn't taken into account was the height of the table. His head connected hard with the underside, the tube made its escape, and Rick collapsed back to the floor, rolling over onto his back and holding his head.

When he opened his eyes, he was staring up at a rain of brassieres and three pairs of silken female legs. The women owners of these were backing away from the table, high heels clicking against the floor, hands tugging at the hems of their skirts as though they'd just seen a rodent on the loose.

Rick pushed himself out and got to his feet, facing the three women from across the table. They were still backing away from the tabletop lingerie display with looks of indignation on their faces. Rick was stammering apologies to them as they exited the shop, the saleswoman was once again laughing hysterically, and Minmei was suddenly behind him, tapping him on the shoulder, soliciting his opinion of the dress she was trying on. He stood shell-shocked for a minute, laughter in one ear, Minmei's questions in the other, and left the store without a word.

Minmei remained inside for well over an hour. She had two additional shopping bags with her when she came out. Undaunted, Rick once again tried to suggest a walk in the park, but she had already made other plans for the two of them. Her surrogate family, who ran Macross City's most popular Chinese restaurant, the White Dragon, had been asking for Rick, and this would be a perfect time to visit—he looked so "gallant and dashing" in his uniform.

Rich could hardly refuse. Minmei's aunt and uncle were almost like family to him; in fact, he had lived with them above the restaurant before joining the Defense Forces.

They were an odd couple—Max, short and portly, and Lena, Minmei's tall and gracious inspiration. They had a son back on Earth, Lynn-Kyle, whom Lena missed and Max preferred not to think about, for reasons Rick hadn't learned. Although there was little else that either kept from him. As Rick entered the restaurant they pretended surprise, but within minutes they had his favorite meal spread out before him. While wolfing down the stir-fried shrimp, he regaled them with the barracks stories he had been saving for Minmei. They wanted to know all about the Veritech fighters—how they handled in deep space, how they were able to switch from Fighter to Guardian or Battloid mode. And they asked about the war: Had Gloval managed to contact Earth headquarters? Did his commanders believe that the enemy would continue their attacks? Was Rick worried about his first mission? How long it would be before the SDF-1 returned to Earth?

Rick did his best to answer them, sidestepping issues he was not permitted to discuss and at other times exaggerating his importance to the Defense Forces. It concerned him that the residents of Macross City were not being given the same reports issued to the Veritech squadrons. After all, Macross was as much a part of the ship and the war as the rest of those onboard.

He was about to allay their fears for his safety by telling them that a combat assignment was far off, when he saw Roy Fokker enter the restaurant. The lieutenant's six-six frame looked gargantuan in the low-ceilinged room, but there was something about Roy's unruly blond hair and innocent grin that put people at ease immediately. He greeted everyone individually, made a show of kissing Minmei's hand, and took a seat next to Rick, snatching up the last of the shrimp as he did so.

"Figured I'd find you here," Roy said with his mouth full. "Gotta get you back to the base on the double, Little Brother."

"Why, what's up?" Rick asked.

"We're on alert."

Rick was suddenly concerned. "Yeah, but what's that have to do with me?"

Roy licked his fingers. "Guess who's been assigned to my squadron?"

Rick was speechless.

Aunt Lena and Uncle Max stood together, worried looks behind the faint smiles. Minmei, however, was ecstatic.

"Oh, Rick, that's wonderful!"

Like he'd just been awarded a prize.

Roy stood up and smiled. "Up and at 'em, partner."

Rick tried valiantly to return a smile that wasn't there. The war had caught up with him again.

CHAPTER
TWO

From the start it was inevitable that a cult should develop around the Veritech fighters. Like the World War I aces, jet fighter jocks, astronauts, and computer linguists before them, the men who were chosen to interact with the first by-product of Robotechnology considered themselves to be at the cutting edge of human progress. And in a sense they were. For who before them had interfaced with machines on such an intimate level? It was only fitting that they should form their own club and speak their own language— call themselves "mechamorphs." They were continually borrowing and applying mystic phrases from their Zen masters—those actually responsible for teaching the pilots the essentials of meditative technique . . . You'd be walking around Macross in those days and hear phrases like "dropping trou" and "standing upright" being tossed about—referring to reconfiguration to Guardian mode and battloid mode, respectively. Pilots would talk to you about your "thinking caps," the sensor-studded helmets worn, or about the thrill of "haloing" (fixing an enemy on target in the mind's eye) or "alpha-bets" (gambling with yourself that you were deep enough in trance for the mecha to understand you) or "facing mecha" (going into battle) or "azending . . ."

Zachary Fox, Jr., *VT: the Men and the Mecha*

GLOVAL MET FREQUENTLY WITH DR. LANG DURING the development phase of what was being called the pinpoint barrier system. The lambent energy that once filled the spacefold generators' chamber had been harnessed and redirected. Such was the nature of this antielectron energy, however, that a photon shield for the entire fortress would have further destabilized an already weakened gravity control system. The best that Lang and his Robotechnicians had been able to come up with was a cluster of movable barriers capable of deflecting incoming bolts. An area aft of the ship's bridge had been retrofitted with three manually operated universal gyros, each tied to one of the cluster's photon discs.

With the barrier system now operational, Captain Gloval was confident that his "Blitzkrieg" attack plan would prove viable. The strategy was simple enough: When the SDF-1 was in close proximity to Saturn's rings, electronic countermeasures would be activated to jam the enemy's radar scanners. The fortress would hide within the rings to take full advantage of their intrinsic radio "noise," while at the same time, squadrons of Veritech fighters would be deployed in a simulated attack mission to act as decoys. When the enemy moved in to engage the VTs, the SDF-1's main gun would take them out. Orbital dynamics would make the timing critical: If the fortress reentered orbit too early, it would be catapulted back toward the outer planets; too late, and the launch window to Mars and the inner planets would be closed.

The VT fighter pilots would receive most of this information at the scheduled briefing, and it was to this briefing that Rick and Roy were headed after they left the restaurant.

Roy had been doing his best to cheer up the newly graduated cadet. Rick was one of five cadets chosen; it was really an honor, an endorsement of his flying skills. He would be able to move out of the dormitory barracks into his own room. There would be more free time, special privileges.

They were walking along the tall chain-link fence that surrounded the barracks compound now. Fifty-foot-tall Battloid sentries patrolled the perimeter, their gatlings shouldered like proper soldiers. Defense Force personnel were moving quickly in response to new orders which had been delivered to each unit.

But Rick's morale was low; his hands were in his pockets, and his shoulders drooped. Roy, however, succeeded in bringing him around with a sharp, "Ten-shun!"

Rick responded expertly to his conditioning: His head came up, he squared his shoulders, brought his back straight, hand at his forehead. His eyes searched for a superior's uniform, but the only people in his field of vision were four young women in civilian dress. The oldest among them, not more than twenty-three or twenty-four herself, was the one who returned his salute. She had thick brown hair coiled at her shoulders, small, attractive features, and an athletic body even her conservative outfit couldn't conceal. There was an air of cool command about her.

The other three were suddenly laughing and pointing at him; the tall, dark-haired one—Kim, Rick understood —was whispering something to the one with glasses— Vanessa. Rick was resisting an urge to check his fly buttons, when the short blonde among them yelled, "Mr. Lingerie!"

He decided to risk a full look and recognized three of the women from this morning's incident in the dress shop. One of them was saying, "Hold your skirts down, ladies," and Roy was elbowing him in the ribs.

"What gives, Little Brother?"

"Don't ask," Rick said out of the corner of his mouth.

The oldest had stepped forward; she gave Rick a look and turned to Roy.

"Commander Fokker, don't tell me this is the *brilliant* new pilot you were raving about?"

"One and the same. Corporal Rick Hunter, this is the Flight Officer Lisa Hayes. You'll be hearing a lot from her from now on."

Rick saluted again. The women were still needling him with comments.

"Rick Hunter..." Lisa Hayes was repeating. "Why does that name sound familiar? Have we met—uh, before this morning, I mean?"

"No, sir, I don't think so, sir."

Lisa tapped her lower lip with her forefinger. She knew that name from somewhere...and all at once she had it: Hunter was the civilian pilot who had shown up at Macross on Launching Day. The same one who had made unauthorized use of a Veritech, the same one who had rescued that Chinese girl, the same one who had called her—

"You're that loudmouthed pilot, aren't you?"

Rick stared at her. Yes, unbelievable as it was, she was the one he had seen on the Veritech commo screen months ago.

"Then you must be—"

"Go ahead, Corporal Hunter, say it: I must be..."

"Y-you must be...my superior officer, sir!"

Lisa smirked and nodded her head knowingly. She motioned to her group, and they started off down the sidewalk. But Lisa turned to Rick as she passed him and added, "By the way, I don't know what your particular problem is, but it's hardly appropriate behavior for a VT pilot to be hanging around lingerie shops looking for a cheap thrill."

Rick groaned. Roy scratched his head. The blonde said: "Creep."

Later, at the briefing, Rick was still replaying the incident; but in light of what was being said, embarrassment placed last on his list of concerns. A decoy mission—the VTs were actually going to pretend to launch a counter-offensive against the aliens! Judging by the murmurs in the crowd, Rick was not the only pilot to be floored by this directive. But like it or not, they had their orders.

"I want you to be thinking of one thing and one thing only," the general was saying. "Robotech! And I want you to know that we're all counting on you."

If the general had let it go at that, Rick would have been all right—afraid but not desperate. The general, however, had then added: "If there's anyone you want to see, you'd better do it tonight."

Rick was in a panic. What did he mean by that—that they were being sent out on some kind of suicide mission? And *do* what tonight—say good-bye, say wish me well, say please remember me always?

He stood on line to use the phone and managed to reach Minmei's aunt Lena. Minmei was at ballet school, but yes, Lena would relay Rick's message: Macross Central Park, their bench at nine P.M.

Rick rode back into the city with a few of the other pilots. He kicked around the market area for a while and was in the park by eight o'clock keeping their bench warm. Starlight poured in from the huge bay in the hull; lovers held one another; life went on as though filled with limitless tomorrows. But Rick couldn't see past the mission, and he was frightened.

By ten o'clock she still hadn't showed; the park was quiet, and he was about to move on. But just then she came running in, face flushed and out of breath.

"Rick, I'm sorry I'm so late."

He smiled at her. "At least you made it."

She pushed her bangs back. Her forehead was beaded with sweat.

"What's the big emergency, anyway?"

"They're sending us out on a mission tomorrow."

He didn't need to add any dramatic accents to it; the words just fell out that way. But her reaction was unexpected. She was practically clapping for him.

"Oh, Rick, that's great! Really, I'm so happy for you!"

And for a moment her enthusiasm almost won him over. *Hey*, Rick told himself, *maybe this is how I'm supposed to feel, like I'm lucky or something*. The park fountain was even gushing in his honor! It didn't last, though, despite her continued exclamations.

"Your first mission! I can't believe it! I'm so proud of you!"

Obviously this was what supporting the war effort was all about, he decided. And she was very good at it.

Then Minmei was suddenly on her toes, twirling around in front of him. "Do you like it? Don't you just love it?" she kept asking. He was puzzled but caught on fast. The dress! The salmon-colored dress she'd picked up that afternoon.

"You look beautiful, Minmei."

She moved in close and made him repeat it.

"Do you mean it, Rick? Am I really beautiful?"

An idea came to him and he signaled to a robo-camera that was making rounds through the park. The stupid thing kept moving in circles, trying to home in on Rick's call, and he finally had to throw a stone at it to get its attention. The cam approached them, asking for money.

"We'll have a picture taken. You'll see how beautiful you are."

Minmei protested some, and the cam uttered some

stock phrases to get them in the proper mood, but eventually they had the print and Minmei was pleased. A smile and a look of concern; Minmei clinging to his arm; the fountain behind them.

Afterward, she talked dance for half an hour; she read him the lyrics of a song she'd composed. Then she had to be going.

"Uncle Max gets mad when I stay out too late. But I'll see you when you get back, Rick. Have a good mission, and remember, I'm very proud of you."

And with that she was gone, leaving him wondering about tomorrow all over again.

He power-walked and jogged for an hour hoping he would exhaust himself and fall into a deep sleep back in the barracks. But sleep didn't seem to be on tonight's agenda; in fact, he couldn't even keep his eyes closed. It was too hot in his bunk, then too cold, there were too many noises in the room, the pillow just wasn't right . . . Finally he sat up and switched on the reading light. He took the park photo and brought it close to his face. Perhaps he could reach her by concentrating on her image; spoken words weren't doing much good.

Minmei was proud of him; earlier that day she'd been upset with him for carrying her shopping bag because the package hid too much of the uniform. Besides, it was wrong for a Veritech fighter pilot to involve himself in such mundane activities. Well, that much was encouraging to Rick because she had really been his motivation for joining up. During the weeks that followed their shared ordeal in that remote part of the ship, he realized that Minmei could never accept an ordinary man as her lover; he would have to be someone who participated in life to the fullest. Someone romantic, adventurous, full of grand dreams and positive hopes for the future—an all-day-long hero who would never fear, never say die. *A special man, a dearest man, someone to share his life with you alone,* as Minmei had herself written it . . . She was like someone who had gone from childhood to maturity without any of the intervening periods of longing or confusion. And even though Rick had saved her life on two occasions and spent two long lost weeks with her, he had yet to prove himself in her eyes. Without joining up there would have been no way for him to display the heroics she craved, no way to individualize himself, no way to accept himself as her equal.

And yet, even having taken those steps, he felt no closer to her than before. Her love had no fixed center; it was spread across the board and parceled out in equal packets for one and all to enjoy. A hero wouldn't even be enough for her because she belonged to everyone. She was more spirit than woman, more dream than reality.

Rick slipped into fitful sleep for a short while, only to have Roy wake him out of it. Fokker was just checking in, reminding him that they had to be up early tomorrow.

"Your first combat mission is always the worst, kid. I sympathize with you. Now, get some sleep—count fanjets or something."

Everyone had such encouraging words: At the briefing they'd been told to wrap up their personal business, and now Roy tells him that tomorrow is going to be *the worst.* Minmei had behaved like a cheerleader, his commanding officer thought him a lecher . . . It had been quite a day.

So Rick actually took Roy's suggestion—he began counting fanjets—although it wasn't sleep he found in the high numbers but an uncomfortable half state where Commander Hayes and the three bridge bunnies mocked him, and the giant enemy soldier he had confronted on Macross Island was reborn to stalk him.

The reveille call came too quickly. Rick felt like one of the walking dead as he gathered up his gear and zombied his way through morning rituals with the other VT pilots. There was a second preflight briefing, more detailed than the first. Then the men were loaded into personnel carriers and conveyed to the *Prometheus*. Roy and Rick's group drove through Macross City, past the park where he and Minmei had been together only hours before. The city was asleep, peacefully, blessedly unaware.

Even before the transport vehicle had come to a halt in the hangar of the supercarrier, pilots were hopping out and rushing toward their propped Veritechs. The Thorclass *Prometheus*—one of two ships that had been caught up in the spacefold and had since been grafted on to the main body of the SDF-1 was like an active hive, and every drone aboard save Rick seemed certain of his or her duty. He lost Roy in the crowds and stood by the transport scanning for a familiar face among those now rushing by him. He recognized Commander Hayes's voice coming through the PA system.

"All Veritechs report for roll call at *Prometheus*... All Veritechs report immediately for roll call at *Prometheus*...Orange, Blue, and Red squadrons will commence flight preparations on second-level afterdeck ...All remaining squadrons prepare for takeoff from preassigned locations...Reactor control, bridge requests status report on first and third plasma shields..."

Suddenly Fokker had him by the arm and was propelling him through the hangar, filling his ears with lastminute instructions and words of advice. He gave Rick a quick embrace when they were alongside Skull Team's twenty-three and was soon swallowed up in the crowds again.

Rick was assisted into the pilot's crane sling by two techs, who also issued him boots, gloves, and a "thinking cap"—a sensor-studded helmet that was in some ways an outgrowth of the Global Civil War "virtual cockpits" and essential for rapport with the mecha.

Rick regarded the plane as he was being lowered into the cockpit module. In Fighter mode, the mecha was similar in appearance to the supersonic jets of the late twentieth century. But in actuality, the Veritechs were as different from those as cars were to horse-drawn wagons. The aliens who had engineered the super dimensional fortress had found a way to *animate* technological creations, and working from examples found onboard the SDF-1, Dr. Lang and his Robotechnicians had been able to fabricate the Veritechs in much the same way—"chips off the old block," as the scientist called the VTs.

Once inside the cockpit, Rick strapped in and donned the helmet; from this point on he was mind-linked to the fighter. There were still plenty of manual tasks to perform, but the central defense capabilities that set the planes apart from their predecessors were directly tied in to the pilots' mecha-will.

The Veritech was fired up now, reflex engines humming, and cat officers were motioning Rick forward. He adjusted the helmet and seat straps and goosed the throttle to position the fighter onto one of the carrier elevators. A second Skull Team VT joined him there.

As the two crafts were lifted to the flight deck, Rick could see the disc of the sun far off to his left. At the end of the hurricane bow was Saturn, impossibly huge. Commander Hayes was once again on the PA and tac net.

"This operation will be directed toward the Cassini Quadrant. All squadrons will wait in the ice fields of the rings for further instructions."

The ice fields of Saturn's rings, Rick repeated to himself.

And he had thought *yesterday* was bad.

CHAPTER
THREE

The so-called Daedalus Maneuver was the first demonstration of what I have termed "mecha-consciousness"—levels beyond the somewhat primitive, almost instinctual modular transformation. The officers of the bridge, along with the engineering section, did little more than offer a prompt to the SDF-1: The dynamics of the maneuver were carried out by the fortress herself, despite claims to the contrary. I, alone, recognized this for what it was—an attempt on the part of the ship to interface with the living units she carried within her ... Later I would overhear someone in the corridor say that "the Daedalus Maneuver (would) go down in the annals of space warfare as a lucky break for an incompetent crew." In point of fact, however, the SDF-1 was able to repeat this "accident" on four separate occasions.

Dr. Emil Lang: Technical Recordings and Notes

"**I**T IS AS YOU PREDICTED, COMMANDER," EXEDORE said as he entered the flagship's command center.

Without a word, Breetai rose from his seat; a wave of his hand and the projecbeam field began to assemble itself. Here was Zor's ship, still in that bizarre configuration, a speck of gleaming metals caught in starlight and silhouetted against the milky white bands and icy rings of the system's sixth planet. Breetai called for full magnification.

"The Micronians have activated electronic countermeasures and are about to enter the rings," Exedore continued. "They are endangering the ship."

"We cannot permit that."

"I have taken the liberty of contacting Commander Zeril."

"Excellent."

A second wave brought Zeril to the screen. He offered a salute.

"My Lord Breetai, we await your instructions."

"The Micronians are laying a trap for us, Commander Zeril. It would suit me to humor them a bit, but I'm concerned about the security of the dimensional fortress. As your scanners will indicate, the enemy has deployed several squadrons of mecha in the hope of luring you to your doom. Send out enough Battlepods to deal with them.

"The Micronian commander will bring his ship from the rings when you are within range of the main gun. I expect you to cripple the fortress before the gun is armed."

"Sir!" said Zeril.

"You understand that the ship is to be disabled, not destroyed. As we speak, relevant data concerning the ship's vulnerable points is being transmitted to your inboard targeting computers. Success, Commander."

"May you win all your battles, sir!"

Zeril's face faded from the field, replaced now by a wide-angle view of the SDF-1 at the perimeter of the ring system. Breetai and his adviser turned their attention to a second monitor where radar scanners depicted the exiting mecha as flashing color-enhanced motes.

"Attacking with such a weak force is completely illogical," Exedore commented. "They seem to have little knowledge of space warfare."

"They have been a planetbound race for too long, Exedore. Caught up in their own petty squabbles with one another."

"Absolutely and totally illogical."

Breetai moved in close to the scanner screen, as if there were some secret message that could be discerned in those flashing lights.

"I don't believe they realize that we are holding back nearly all our forces . . . But this is an excellent opportunity for us to demonstrate just what they're up against."

No sooner had Rick Hunter executed a full roll to avoid colliding with a chunk of ring ice than Commander Lisa Hayes opened the net, her angry face on the commo screen lighting up the Veritech cockpit.

"Skull twenty-three! What in blazes are you doing? Just where were you at the briefing—asleep? I'm getting sick and tired of repeating myself: That kind of stunt flying will give away your position to the enemy! This isn't the time or place for aerobatics, do you copy?!"

"It was just a roll," Rick said in defense of his actions. "I'm not the only one—"

"That'll be enough, Corporal. Follow Skull Leader's instructions, do you copy?"

"All right," he answered sullenly. "I gotcha."

But Hayes wasn't finished, not by a long shot.

"Is that the way you address superiors, Hunter? Look around you, bright boy. Everyone else here flies by the rules."

"Roger, roger, Commander, I copy."

"And get your RAS back where it belongs—why are you dropping behind?"

"Hey, you're not flying around up here—" He caught himself and made a new start. "Uh, Skull twenty-three increasing relative airspeed, Commander."

Hayes signed off, and Rick breathed a sigh of relief. This was going to be even more difficult than he had imagined. His first mission, and already he was being razzed by some know-it-all bridge bunny. Just his luck! What did she think, it was easy out here? *Oh, to be back in the* Mockingbird, Rick thought.

They were flying blind in Saturn's shadow, far from the surface of the rapidly spinning planet and deep in the ice fields of its outermost rings. Rick's eyes were glued to the cockpit screens and displays, and yet even with all this sophisticated instrumentation he had already had several close calls with debris too insignificant to register on the short-range scanners but large enough to inflict damage. He knew that the rest of Skull Team was out there somewhere, but visual contact would have been reassuring right about now—a glimpse of thruster fire, a glint of sunlight on a wingtip, anything at all. Soon enough there would be an added element of danger—the arrival of the enemy Battlepods.

Just then, Roy Fokker appeared on the port commo screen.

"Get ready, fellas, here they come."

There's no more flying for fun.

Claudia Grant, the black Flight Officer on the SDF-1's bridge, was monitoring Lisa Hayes's conversation with the young VT pilot when radar informed her of the enemy's counterattack.

Claudia and Lisa had adjacent stations along the curved forward hull of the bridge, beneath the main wraparound bays which now afforded views of the rocks and ice chunks that made up Saturn's rings. Each woman had two overhead monitors and a console screen at her disposal. Elevated behind Lisa's post was the command chair, and behind the captain along the rear bulkheads on either side of the hatch sat Sammie and Kim, each duty station equipped with nine individual screens that formed a grand square. Vanessa was off to starboard, positioned in front of the ten-foot-high threat board.

Claudia's station was linked to those of the three junior officers by radio, but such was her proximity to Lisa's that scarcely a word the commander uttered escaped her hearing. Not that there would have been anything left unshared between them in any case. They had forged a close friendship; Claudia, four years Lisa's senior, often playing the role of older sister, especially in matters of the heart. But for of all her desirable traits, her natural attractiveness and keen intelligence, Lisa was emotionally inexperienced. She projected an image of cool and capable efficiency, rationalizing her detached stance in the name of "commitment to duty." But buried in her past was an emotional wound that had not yet healed. Claudia knew this much, and she hoped to help Lisa exorcise that demon some day. This new VT pilot, Hunter, had touched something deep inside Lisa by calling her just as he had seen her—"that old sourpuss"—and Claudia wanted to press her friend for details. But this was hardly the time or the place.

"Enemy Battlepods now engaging our Veritechs in the Cassini Quadrant, Captain," Claudia relayed.

"Enemy destroyer approaching the target zone," Vanessa added.

Gloval rubbed his hands together and rose from his chair.

"Excellent. If we can get a visual on the destroyer, I want it on the forward screen. Let's see what these ships look like."

Sammie punched it up, and soon the entire bridge crew was staring at the enemy vessel. It was surely as large as if not larger than the SDF-1, perhaps two and a half kilometers in length, but in no other way similar to it. Broad and somewhat flat, the warship had a vaguely organic look, enhanced by the dark green color of its dorsal armored shells and the light gray of its seemingly more vulnerable underbelly. Oddly enough, it also appeared to be quilled; but there was good reason to suspect that many of those spines were weapons.

"Not a pretty sight, is she?" said Gloval.

"Sir," said Vanessa, "the destroyer is within range."

"All right. Bring the ship around to the predesignated coordinates. Make certain there are no fluctuations in the barrier system readings and prepare to fire the main gun on my command."

Claudia tapped in the coordinates. She could feel the huge reflex-powered thrusters kick in to propel the ship away from Saturn's gravitational grasp. The pinpoint barrier system checked out, and the main gun was charging.

Free of the rings now, the SDF-1 was repositioning itself. The twin main gun towers were leveling out from the shoulders of the ship, taking aim at a target hundreds of kilometers away.

"Main gun locked on target, sir."

Gloval's fist slammed into his open hand. "Fire!"

Claudia pushed down a series of crossbar switches, threw open a red safety cover, and pressed home the firing device.

Illumination on the bridge failed momentarily.

The gun did not fire.

Again Claudia tapped in a series of commands; there was no response.

"Quickly!" Gloval shouted. "Get me Lang."

"On the line," Kim said.

Lang's thickly accented voice resounded through the bridge comlink speakers.

"Captain, the pin-point barrier is apparently interfering with the main gun energy transformers. We're doing a vibrational analysis now, but I don't think we'll have use of the gun unless we scrap the shield power."

"Bozhe moy!" said Gloval in his best Russian.

Sammie swiveled from her console to face the captain, "Sir, particle-beam trackers are locked on our ship. The enemy is preparing to fire!"

Eight weeks of special training had failed to prepare him for the silent insanity of space warfare. Disintegration and silent death, the pinpoints of distant light that were laser beams locked on to his ship, the stormy marriage of antiparticles, the grotesque beauty of short-lived spherical explosions—bolts of launched lightning, blue and white, igniting the proper combination of gases . . .

Rick Hunter fired the VT's thrusters as two Battlepods closed in on him from above—the relative "above" at any rate, for there was no actual up or down out here, no real way to gauge acceleration except by the constant force that kept him pinned to the back of his seat, or pushed him forward when the retros were kicked in, no way to judge velocity except in relation to other Veritech fighters or the SDF-1 herself. Just that unvarying starfield, those cool and remote fires that were the backdrop of war.

It was said that the best VT pilots were those who simply allowed themselves to forget: about yesterday, today, or tomorrow. *"Nothing extraneous, in mind or body."* Warfare in deep space was a silent Zen video game where victory was not the immediate goal; success to any degree depended on a clear mind, free of expectations, and a body conditioned for thoughtless reaction. Stop to think about where to place your shot, how to move or mode your mecha, and you were space debris. Fight the fear and you'd soon be sucking vacuum. Rather, you had to embrace the terror, pull it down into your guts and let it free your spirit. It was like forcing yourself through the climax of a nightmare, confronting there all the worst things that could happen, then piercing through the envelope into undreamed-of worlds. And the dreamstate was the key, because you had to believe you had complete control of each detail, every element. The silence of space was the perfect medium for this manipulated madness. Out here, content was more important than form; wings were superfluous, banking and breaks unnecessary, thoughts dangerous.

Rick knew when he was trying too hard: He would feel the alpha vibe abandon him and the mecha follow suit. *You are the mecha, the mecha is you.* Left empty, the fear would rush in to fill him up, like air rushing into a vacuum, and the fear would trigger a further retreat from the vibe. It was a vicious circle. But he was beginning to recognize the early stages of it, the waverings and oscillations, and that in itself represented an all-important first step.

He stayed at Fokker's wing, learning from him. The pods were not as maneuverable as the Veritechs and nowhere near as complex. They also had far more vulnerable points. It was just that there were so damned many of them. One Battlepod, one enemy pilot. How strong was their number? How long could they keep this up?

Rick came to Roy's aid whenever he could, using

heat-seekers and gatling, saving the undercarriage lasers for close-in fighting.

The assault group had fought its way out of the rings and shadow zone, but not without devastating losses to the Red and Green teams. And the SDF-1 had still not fired the main gun.

It was difficult to tell just what was going on back at the fortress. Rick could see that it was taking heavy fire from the enemy destroyer, a bizarre-looking ship if ever he'd seen one: a cross between a manta ray and a mutant cucumber. But for some reason the enemy was using rather conventional ordnance, easily thwarted by the fortress's movable shields. It would only be a matter of time before the destroyer upped the ante.

Rick guessed Command's new orders for Skull Team long before Roy appeared on the screen with them: The VTs were to attack the destroyer.

Fokker led them in, searching for soft spots in the forest-green hull. Battlepods continued to exit the ship through semicircular topside portals, so the Skull Leader directed the attack along the underside of the destroyer, using everything his fighter was prepared to deliver.

Rick had completed one pass, discharging half his remaining Stilettos. He was preparing for a second run now, coming in across the nose of the destroyer this time, zeroing in on two massive cannons set close to the central ridge. Suddenly a Battlepod streaked in front of him with a VT in close pursuit; the mecha let loose a flock of heat-seekers which caught up with the pod directly over Rick's fighter. He dropped the VT into a nose dive, expecting concussion where there was none, then executed two rollovers but still couldn't manage to pull the mecha out of its collision course with the destroyer. Desperately, he reached out for the mode levers and reconfigured to Guardian. This would at least enable him to extend the "legs" of the mecha and utilize the foot thrusters to brake his speed. But the angle of his approach was too critical. With the nose beginning to dip and the energized foot thrusters threatening to throw him into a roll, Rick again switched modes, this time to Battloid configuration. Regardless, he was committed to completing the front flip, and the Battloid came down with a silent crash, face first on the armored hull.

As on the SDF-1's shell, there was artificial gravity here, but Rick had no time to be impressed: two Battlepods were on him, coming in fast now for strafing runs. He thought the mecha to a kneeling position and brought the gatling cannon out front. Blue bolts from the pods were striking the hull around him, fusing metals and blowing slag into the void. It didn't seem to bother the enemy pilots any that they were firing on their own ship; they were intent on finishing him off, homing in now, bipedal legs dangling and plastron cannons firing like spheroid kamikazes.

Rick was backing away from blue lightning, returning continuous fire. The big gun was dangerously close to overheating in the Battloid's hands.

Then, suddenly, the hull seemed to give way under him. Instantly Rick realized that he had stumbled the Battloid through one of the topside semicircular ports.

The mecha landed on its butt, twenty-five meters below the action on the floor of a loading bay. Rick worked the foot pedals frantically, raising the Battloid to its feet in time to see the overhead hatch close—a shot from one of the pods had probably activated the external control circuitry. There was a second hatch in the bay which undoubtedly led to the innards of the destroyer.

Rick began to approach this second hatch cautiously,

studying the air lock entry controls and feeling strangely secure in the sealed chamber. Just then the air lock door slid open. On the other side of the threshold stood an enemy soldier who had apparently heard Rick's fall to the floor. He was easily as tall as the Battloid and massively built; but although he was armored, his head was bare and he was weaponless.

The alien goliath and the small human in the cockpit of the mecha had taken each other by surprise. As dissimilar as these potential combatants were, their frightened reactions were the same. The defenseless soldier's eyes darted left and right, desperately seeking an escape route as Rick's did the same. The alien warrior then stepped back, body language betraying his thoughts.

It was all that was needed to break the stalemate: Rick raised the muzzle of the Battloid's gatling, metal-shod fingers poised on the trigger.

The enemy destroyer was bearing down on the SDF-1, peppering her with hundreds of missiles. Radar scanners located throughout the body of the fortress relayed course headings of the incoming projectiles to inboard computers, which in turn translated the data into colored graphics. These displays were flashed to monitors in the barrier control room, where three young female techs worked feverishly to bring photon disc cover to projected impact points, the spherical gyros of the pin-point barrier system spinning wildly under the palms of their hands.

On the bridge Captain Gloval feared the worst. The main gun was still inoperable, and despite the effectiveness of the shields, the ship was sustaining damage on all sides. Skull Team was counterattacking the destroyer, but it was unlikely they'd be able to inflict enough damage to incapacitate it. Was there ever in Earth's history a commander who had more than 50,000 civilian lives at stake in one battle? For all these long months Gloval had never once contemplated surrender. Now, however, he found that possibility edging into his thoughts, draining him of strength and will.

As if reading Gloval's thoughts, Lisa suddenly came up with an inspired plan. But first she needed to know if it was possible to concentrate and direct the pin-point barrier energy to the front of the *Daedalus*—the super-carrier that formed the right arm of the SDF-1.

Gloval immediately contacted Dr. Lang, and the reply came swiftly: Yes, it could be done.

Gloval ordered him to begin the energy transfer at once and quickly set in motion phase two of the plan. This required that all available Destroids, Spartans, and Gladiators—the "ground" support weapons mecha—be gathered together at the bow of the *Daedalus*. The final phase would be handled by the Captain himself; he reassumed the command chair, his strength and confidence renewed.

"Ramming speed," he ordered. "We're going to push the *Daedalus* right down their throat!"

Members of the Skull Team who took part in Operation Blitzkrieg would later report on the spectacle they witnessed that day in Saturn space. How the SDF-1, gleaming blue, red, and white, engulfed in explosions and locked on a collision course with the enemy, had executed a backward body twist, followed by a full-forward thrust of its right arm that brought the bow of the *Daedalus* like a battering ram squarely into the forward section of the destroyer.

One can only imagine the scene from Commander Zeril's point of view: the impact; the sight of the front of his ship being splintered apart, cables and conduits rupturing as the destroyer impaled itself on the arm of the fortress; stressed metal groaning and giving way, crossties and girders ripped from their lodgings; the mad rush of precious air being sucked from the ship.

Perhaps Zeril and his second were alive long enough to see the forward ramp of the *Daedalus* drop open, revealing row after row of deadly Destroids, thick with guns, missile tubes, and cannons. Perhaps the two Zentraedi even saw the initial launch of the five thousand projectiles fired into the heart of the destroyer, the first series of explosions against the hull and bulkheads of the bridge.

Rick couldn't bring himself to waste the enemy soldier. His mind and trigger finger were paralyzed, not out of fear but forgiveness. This was no Battlepod he was face to face with in the air lock but a living, breathing creature, caught up just as Rick in the madness of war. *Remember what they did to us at Macross Island*, Roy had drilled into him. *Remember! Remember!* ... humankind's war cry for how many millenia now? And when would it end—with this war? the next? the one after that?

Suddenly the soldier turned his head sharply to the right, as though he had heard something unreported by the Battloid's sensors. Rick saw the soldier's face drain of color, his eyes go wide with even greater fear.

In the next instant a conflagration swept through the corridor. The soldier was vaporized before Rick's eyes, and the Battloid was thrown back into the loading bay by the explosive force of the firestorm. The air lock was sealed, but the chamber walls were already beginning to melt.

Rick brought the Battloid's top-mounted lasers into action to melt through the overhead latch controls, and soon enough the semicircular hatch slid open. Foot thrusters blazing, the mecha rose from the floor and clambered out onto the destroyer's outer skin.

The ship was convulsing beneath Rick, disgorging a death rattle roar from its holds. Forward, he could see the SDF-1 propelling itself away from the crippled enemy, its pectoral boosters blowtorching and its *Daedalus* right arm flayed of metal and superstructure.

Rick returned the mecha to Guardian for his takeoff, then well into the launch he reconfigured to Fighter mode, kicking in the afterburners to carry him away from the destroyer.

A series of enormous blisters was forming along the outer shell of the ship as explosive fire launched by the Destroids was funneled front to stern. But the hull could contain it for only so long; the pustules began to burst, loosing coronas and prominences of radiant energy into the void. A violent interior explosion then blasted the destroyer's skin from its framework. At last there was nothing left but a self-consuming glowing cloud, a war of gases bent on mutual annihilation. The energy flourished wildly and dispersed, leaving in the end no trace of itself nor its brief struggle.

CHAPTER
FOUR

*Several historians of the Robotech Wars—Rawlins,
Daily, Gordon, and Turno, to name but a few—have advanced the claim that it was Breetai's decision [to call up
Khyron's troops as reinforcements] that placed the Zentraedi squarely on the road to defeat. Rawlins, in his two-
volume study,* Zentraedi Triumvirate: Dolza, Breetai,
Khyron, *states: "It was more than a tactical blunder . . .
Khyron's use of the dried leaves of the Invid Flower of Life
had drastically affected his Zentraedi conditioning. Subsequent research clearly demonstrated that alkaloids present
in the leaves had a direct effect on the limbic system of the
brain. The Flower had the power to stimulate a resurgence
of archaic patterns of behavior. In the case of the Zentraedi,
ironically enough, those behavior patterns were the ones
which most clearly defined the human condition . . . So in
this sense it may be said that Khyron was the most human of
them all."*

History of the First Robotech War, Vol. XXXIV

BREETAI WAS NOW BEGINNING TO ENJOY THIS Micronian battle game.

" 'Cat and mouse' did you call it?"

"Yes, my lord. Apparently it refers to a game the
stronger animal plays with the weaker before the final
kill."

"Excellent. You must teach me their language, Exedore."

"Of course, sir. It is most primitive, easy to absorb.

Our three operatives from surveillance are making rapid progress."

"Yes . . . I may want to talk to these Micronians soon."

The flagship and several of the fleet's scout and recon ships had made a hyperspace jump along the projected course of the SDF-1. Breetai had left behind several cruisers and destroyers, along with plenty of Battlepods, to keep the Micronians busy while he plotted his next move in the game.

The Zentraedi commander smiled wryly as he viewed the trans-vids of Zeril's destruction. Enhanced-motion playback had captured the giant ship's final few moments splendidly. He had to credit the Micronians for the unorthodox nature of their counterattack. Instead of further depleting their power by firing the main gun, they had used one of their oceangoing vessels to ram Zeril's destroyer headlong. Once inside, a sufficient amount of firepower must have been unleashed to destroy it. The ship blistered, glowed, became a veritable tunnel of trapped photon energy, and exploded.

Yes, Breetai was amused by the challenge of illogical behavior; it forced him to step outside his own conditioning and search for novel approaches to destruction.

His thoughts were now interrupted by a communiqué from astrogation. Exedore relayed the message.

"Sir, emerging from hyperspace-fold."

The composite projecbeam disassembled itself. Exedore called for an exterior view of local space. Cameras panned across the unbroken blackness and locked on a small red planet, arid and angry-looking. For Breetai it brought to mind memories of Fantoma, and the mining worlds he had worked and patrolled long ago. A schematic appeared on one of the side screens of the command bowl showing the planetary system of this yellow star the Micronians referred to as their "sun."

"Mars," said Exedore, "the fourth planet."

Breetai turned to his adviser.

"Has the recon vessel been deployed?"

"As you ordered, sir. The Cyclops transmissions are coming in now."

The projecbeam revealed an abandoned Micronian base that showed signs of an earlier battle: craters from explosions covered with the fine red swirling dust of the planet's deserts, a shuttlecraft disabled and still in its launch bay, the shells of buildings and fractured domes.

"Our scanners reveal no life readings, no energy levels of any form save minimal low-level background radiation, Commander."

Breetai put his massive hand to his head and unconsciously stroked the metal plate there. The plate concealed scar tissue that had overgrown the wounds received while protecting Zor from the Invid; now, it seemed, each time he came close to fulfilling his imperative—to capture the fortress—the original pain returned.

"It would appear that the Earth people abandoned this installation."

Exedore studied the data screen. "Long-range surface scanners indicate that a military conflict took place here and at a neighboring installation. Nevertheless, the Micronians' reflex power furnaces are still operative, and we've managed to tap into their computer banks and access some of the information. It seems that most of the inhabitants, sir, were destroyed in a battle with their allied forces, and the few that survived were unable to escape the harshness of the planet itself."

Breetai continued to stroke his faceplate. "Hmmm

... see to it that one of the computers is activated and the contents of its memory transmitted on a hailing frequency."

One of Exedore's eyebrow's arched. "Certainly, my lord, but why?"

"Because this abandoned post will make a perfect trap. I have ordered the Seventh Mechanized Division of the Botoru Battalion to assemble here immediately."

The Seventh had a reputation for ground-based savagery and more.

"Impossible," said Exedore with alarm. "Surely, sir, this cannot be; you haven't ordered up *Khyron's* division?"

Breetai smiled bemusedly at his companion. "Indeed I have, and why not?"

"You're familiar with his battle record, his reputation."

"What of it?"

"During the Mona Operation, he was intoxicated and ended up killing some of his own men." Exedore pressed his point. "And in the Isyris battle zone he almost wiped out two divisions of friendly forces—"

"While successfully destroying the enemy."

"True, sir, but because of that his own troops have named him the 'Backstabber.'"

Breetai was about to respond, when without warning the bridge went on alert. Lights began to flash, and warning klaxons were sounding general quarters. Exedore had already positioned himself at the control pads of one of the monitors, trying to ascertain the cause. Breetai stood over him now as data began to flash across the screens.

"What is it?" the commander demanded.

"Armed ships emerging from hyperspace in the midst of our battle group. A collision appears imminent!"

Breetai turned to the forward projecbeam. "Some of the Micronians' unorthodoxy!"

A card player at a show of hands, Breetai readied himself, fully expecting the materialization of a squadron of Micronian mecha. But what appeared instead were the ragtag ships of the Botoru Battalion.

Visual distortions in local space preceded their crazed arrival, shimmerings and oscillations in the fabric of real time. Several vessels of Khyron's battle group collided with ships of the main fleet, spreading shock waves throughout the field. Even the flagship itself was rocked by debris, the force of the impact strong enough to knock Exedore off his feet. Damage reports were pouring in to the bridge; debris appeared in the projecbeam field.

Exedore picked himself up; his voice was full of anger when he spoke.

"This is happening just as I expected! Khyron, sir, is totally without discipline!"

Was this an oversight, Breetai asked himself, *or just a demonstration of Khyron's recklessness*?

The Backstabber's face suddenly appeared on the forward screen. Khyron, long steel-blue hair falling over the collar of a uniform of his own design, saluted. His face was a curious mixture of boyish innocence and brooding anger, Prince Valiant's devilish shadow with a fire in his eyes that was not quite Zentraedi.

"Commander of the Seventh Mechanized Space Division reporting as ordered." His lowered salute turned into a mock wave. "Good to see you again, Commander Breetai." He finished off with a laugh.

"The sheer audacity—" Exedore started to say.

A square-jawed battle-scarred warrior had appeared by Khyron's side in the projecbeam field, sharing some sort of joke with him. "Ha! Just as I thought, Khyron. We crashed into four ships total."

Khyron tried to silence him, but it was too late.

"You thought it would be three at best. I win the bet."

"Be quiet, you fool," ordered Khyron finally. "Our conversation is being broadcast."

Breetai fixed him with his one eye. "Khyron, don't trifle with me if you value your command. I'm willing to give you a chance to make up for your past mistakes, but I have no time for your games. Is that understood?"

Khyron straightened his smile, but the laughter remained in his eyes. "Yes, Commander, what is it you want me to do?"

"There's an abandoned base on the fourth planet of this star system. We intend to lure Zor's ship there, and I want you to see to it that it doesn't leave. Trap it with gravity mines if you have to, but understand this: Your Seventh will blockade the ship without damaging it unduly. You will then await my further instructions. Is that clear? You are to await my instructions before engaging the enemy."

"Perfectly clear, Breetai. I would naturally prefer you to have the honor and glory of the capture. Commander-in-Chief Dolza expects nothing less of you, I'm sure."

"That will be enough, Khyron," said Exedore.

Breetai gestured to his adviser. "Send out a recall order to our Battlepods. Let's give the Micronians enough breathing room to take the bait we're going to lay out for them."

Khyron signed off. Exedore continued to plead the case against using him, but Breetai was already looking forward to the plan. The prospect of a trap excited him.

Furthermore, real sport required the unexpected, and in this contest for Zor's ship and the precious cargo it held, Khyron would play the Zentraedi's wild card.

Two Battlepods were right on his tail, pouring fire into the mecha. Rick didn't need gauges to feel the lock of those lasers; they might as well have been burning into his skull. He opened up the gap somewhat by hitting his afterburners, then tacked toward relative-twelve and waited for the pods to split up. He knew they'd attempt to pinch him, but he had plans of his own.

Rick took his mind off the pod below him. He had number one haloed in his rear sights. Firing the forward retros to cut his velocity, he loosed a cluster of heat-seekers. The missiles tore from beneath the right wing of the mecha and accelerated into a vertical climb, homing in on the enemy ship. Rick used the port thrusters to angle himself free of the debris and risked a brief look up and over his shoulder. The rockets caught the Battlepod in the belly, blowing off both legs and cracking the spherical hull.

Scratch one.

Number two was still below him, trying to roast the underside of Rick's mecha with continuous heat. A little more of this and he'd be cooked. Lateral swings were getting him nowhere, so he thought the fighter into a rapid dive, rolling over as he fell. The enemy lasers were now tickling the back of the Veritech, and Rick had to act fast: He returned fire with is own top-mounted guns, training them on the hinge straps of the pod's chestplate.

The enemy pilot understood Rick's move and arced his guns toward the more vulnerable cockpit of the mecha. But he was too late; the hinges of the chestplate slagged out, and the pod opened up like a newly hatched egg. Rick caught a glimpse of the giant flailing around in his cockpit before he completed his roll and engaged the boosters.

Scratch two.

He was headed away from the fortress now. The scene before him had to have been lifted from some nightmare: Space was alive with swarms of Battlepods . . . photon beams laced through the blackness, and silent explosions brought the colors of death and destruction to an indifferent universe.

For three days now the pods had pressed their attack. There had been little sleep for the Robotech forces, even less for the SDF-1 flight crews. After the *Daedalus* Maneuver and their success in the rings of Saturn, there was some hope that the enemy had for once suffered a setback. And for almost a month, while the fortress crossed the Jovian orbit and the asteroid belt, there were no attacks. But that period of calm was behind them.

Captain Gloval and Dr. Lang had reversed the modular transformation and disassembled the pin-point barrier system in an attempt to arm the main gun once again, but their efforts had proved futile. For the rest, the still slightly shell-shocked masses of displaced persons of Macross city, catapulted like himself from the southern Pacific to the icy regions of deep space, there was nothing to do but adjust to the reality of the situation, continue to rebuild lives and the city itself. Every now and again, they could marvel at the wonders of space travel, the stark and silent beauty of it, and forget for a moment that they were not tourists out here but unwilling players in a nonstop game of death, pursued by the seemingly limitless forces of a race of giant warrior beings who had dropped out of the skies and turned the world upside down.

Only a month before, Rick had been face to face with one of those titans in an air lock on one of the alien ships. He recalled staring out of the cockpit of the transformed Veritech at the giant, who at first had openly feared him, then cursed and ridiculed him for not having the will to blast him away. The laughter of that alien still rang in his ears, followed by his guilt and confusion.

But most of all the memory of the giant's fiery death.

How could one ever forget?

Two Battlepods were suddenly behind him, looking for laser lock. Rick executed a double rollover and dive to lose them. Peripherally, he saw the Blue Team leader swoop in and take them out.

"Way to go Blue Leader!" Rick shouted into the tac net.

"Just do the same for me sometime, buddy," came the reply.

"You got it."

Rick and the Blue Leader, wing to wing, led a frontal assault on yet another enemy wave. They launched themselves into the thick of it, dispatching several of the enemy. Lateral thrusters took them out of the arena momentarily, and the SDF-1 came into view, her main batteries, Phalanx guns, and Gladiator mecha issuing steady fire. The fortress, enveloped by a swarm of pods, looked as though it had somehow wandered into a fireworks display.

Commander Hayes was calling for an assist in Fifth Quadrant, and Skull and Blue Teams were ordered to respond. Rick and Blue Leader were initiating course corrections when five pods appeared on Rick's radar screen. Three of them were quickly dispatched by Roy Fokker in Skull One, but the remaining two were hounding Blue Leader's VT with a vengeance. The enemy unleashed a massive volley of rockets that caught the mecha broadside. For a moment Blue Leader seemed to hang in space; then the fighter exploded and disintegrated, its parts scattered, its pilot a memory.

Rick turned his face away from the wreckage. *I could be next*, he thought.

How could one ever forget?

The pods continued to press their attack.

Death had a free hand.

Then, as suddenly as they had appeared they were gone. The fighting was over and recall orders came in from the bridge.

Rick followed Roy Fokker's lead into the docking bays of the *Prometheus*.

Roy caught up with him in the hangar and slapped him on the shoulder.

"You looked good up there, Rick. Keep it up."

Rick grunted, removed his helmet, and kept walking, increasing his pace.

Roy caught up with him again. "You can't let it get you down, kid. We sent them home, didn't we?"

Rick turned and confronted his friend. "If you believe that, you're a bigger idiot than I am, Roy."

Roy draped his arm around Rick's shoulders and leaned in. "Listen to me. You're beat. We all are. Get yourself into town after the debriefing. I'm sure Minmei would like to see you."

"That would be a surprise," Rick said, and stormed off.

* * *

Monorail lines now ran from the *Prometheus* and *Daedalus* arms into Macross. A central monorail line ran through the body of the fortress, through enormous interior holds originally meant for creatures ten times human scale—a vast forbidden zone only a portion of which was understood by Dr. Lang's teams of scientists —and through that area where Rick and Minmei had passed two weeks together deep beneath the present streets of the city.

Each passing day brought changes here. There was even talk of using EVE, enhanced video emulation, to bring sunrise and sunset, blue skies and clouds, to the place. Already there was a grid of streets, carefully arranged according to the dictates of the modular transformation schematic, multiple-storied dwellings, shops and restaurants, a central marketplace, even a few banks and a post office.

The city went on living through the war, almost oblivious to it except when energy drains through diversion led to power shortages or when the enemy fighters and Battlepods scored direct hits. Even the ubiquitous uniforms didn't signal war—uniforms were worn by everyone to denote job and detail, a carryover from the island where most of these same people had been connected in one way or another to the reconstruction of the SDF-1. A public address system kept the residents of the city informed about the ship's course through the solar system but was seldom used to report accurate battle results. In fact, it was speaking to the population now, as Rick meandered in vague fashion toward the Chinese restaurant, hoping for an *accidental* encounter with Minmei. Passersby paid the message little mind, but it caught him off guard.

"News from the bridge: We have been attacked by one hundred twenty enemy pods, but our first, fourth, and seventh fighter squadrons have succeeded in completely destroying them. Our casualties have been light, and our astrogational system has not been affected. That is all."

Incredible! Rick thought. He was looking around for someone to talk to, someone he could grab by the lapels and awaken with the truth, when an arm caught hold of his. He turned and found himself looking into Minmei's blue eyes.

"Hello, stranger," she said. "I've been worried about you."

She embraced him like a brother.

He had rehearsed how he was going to play this, but standing here with her now, the half-truths from the bridge echoing inside him, he just wanted to hold and protect her. But he managed to keep some distance, and she caught his mood.

He explained about the announcement. "It wasn't true, Minmei. They're misleading everyone. We didn't hit half of them, and our losses were—"

She put a finger to his lips and looked around. "I don't think it's a good idea to talk about this here, Rick."

He broke from her hold. "Listen, Minmei—"

"Besides, everyone's doing all they can for the war effort, and I don't think you'll accomplish anything by getting them—or me—depressed. Especially with my birthday right around the corner."

He could only stare at her and wonder where her

mind was, but she was way ahead of him already. She smiled and took hold of his arm.

"Come on, Rick. Let's get something to eat. Please?"

He gave in. How could he make her understand how it was out there? In here she was doing what they all were: going on with life as if nothing had happened, as if this were home, as if there were a wonderfully blue ocean just over that rise. As if there were no war out there.

On the bridge of the SDF-1 there was little else but war to talk or think about.

Captain Gloval removed his cap and ran a hand through his salt-and-pepper hair. What were the aliens planning now? Obviously their constant attacks were not meant to turn the tide but to wear him down, perhaps in the hope that the SDF-1 would be surrendered. The attacks were like sparring matches; it was as if the enemy was feeling him out, trying to gain some insight into his tactics. Psychological warfare conducted with an inexhaustible supply of ships and no regard for the pilots who flew them. Gloval wondered what his counterpart might look like, what kind of being he was. He recalled the video warning the fortress had broadcast to his small band of explorers some ten years ago . . . One thing was becoming clear: The aliens did not want to damage the SDF-1. They hoped to recapture it intact.

The attacks had thrown them drastically off course, and although closing in on Earth's orbit, they had months of travel ahead of them.

Gloval asked for information about the aliens' retreat. The only thing Claudia and Lisa could be certain of was that there were no longer any traces of enemy pods on the radar screens. Gloval was pondering this when Kim

Young announced that incoming data was being received on one of the open frequencies.

Gloval stepped down from his chair and walked over to take a look at the transmissions.

"... 'If mice could swim,'" he read, "'they would float with the tide and play with the fish. Down by the seaside, the cats on the shore would quickly agree...' What is this nonsense? Where is it coming from?"

Vanessa Leeds tapped in a set of requests and swiveled in her seat to study a secondary monitor. In a moment she had the answer. "A transmitter located sixteen degrees off our current course."

"That would put it at Sara Base on Mars!" said Claudia.

Lisa Hayes turned from her post in a start. "What?! That's impossible! Are you certain of those readings?"

"Sara Base is deserted," said Gloval. "All life there was wiped out during the war. It just can't be."

Lisa and Claudia exchanged a conspiratorial look.

"No, Lisa," said Claudia. "Don't get your hopes up."

"Why couldn't there be survivors?" Lisa said excitedly. She turned to Gloval. "Isn't it possible, sir?"

Gloval crossed his arms, "I don't see how, but it was a pretty big base, and I suppose anything is possible. We've all seen enough lately to convince me of that."

"We have secondary confirmation on the origin of the transmissions, sir. The origin is definitely Sara."

Claudia said, "Perhaps we should check it out, Captain. It would only mean a minor deviation in our course." Again she and Lisa exchanged looks.

Gloval returned to his chair. He thought it unlikely that there were survivors on the base. And the possibility of an enemy trap had to be considered. But there were no radar indications of activity in the area, and the risk presented by a landing would certainly be justified if they could manage to replenish their rapidly diminishing supplies. It would be the last chance until Earthspace, and who knew when that might be. *If* that would be . . .

Gloval turned to his crew.

"How badly hurt are we?"

Vanessa responded, "Astrogation and engineering sections report limited damage only, sir."

"All right," said Gloval. "Change course and head for Mars."

> *The destruction of Sara Base on Mars was in some ways typical of the setbacks experienced by the newly formed World Unification Alliance, the unfortunate result of suspicion, misinformation, and manipulation by an unnamed collective of separatist factions. That the Northeast Asian Co-Prosperity Sphere could be so easily duped into believing the base a military installation was all the more cause for concern. But more than that, the attack upon the base marked the first instance that humankind had taken warfare off the planet and brought it to the stars.*

> Malachi Cain, *Prelude to Doomsday: A History of the Global Civil War*

ARS!

Lisa stared at the barren world as it came into view through the forward bays. Arid, lifeless, named for the ancient god of war, it was like an angry red wound in her heart. Eight years earlier her love had died here, on this world that she was destined to visit, one that had visited her so often in tear-filled dreams. But even so she couldn't suppress the belief, the hope, that one of the many survival scenarios she had played endlessly through these lost years would run to completion. The last time she had seen and held Karl Riber was the evening he had told her of his assignment to Mars Base Sara.

"The Visitor" had crash-landed on Macross Island three years earlier, and the Internationalists—men like her father, Admiral Hayes, Senator Russo, Gloval, and the rest—were doing their best to bring about world unity, centered on the restoration of the SDF-1 and the potential threat to Earth posed by the arrival of that ship built by an advanced race of intellectual and physical giants. But peace and unity were not so easily secured. Factionalism was rampant and borders changed overnight, sides were drawn and redrawn, bombs were dropped, and the killing continued unabated.

She had known Karl only a short time but had loved him from the start. He had been assigned to her father as an aide and was doing his best to be the soldier Admiral Hayes expected at his side. But through and through Karl was a peace-loving man, a sensitive scholar who, like others of his type, was looking forward to a day when the bloodshed would end and humankind would begin to focus itself on its destiny, its true place among the stars. The arrival of the SDF-1 had further inflamed his passion for peace; but when even that event failed to put an end to the reigning madness, there was nothing left for him but cynicism and the need to escape.

That farewell night found Karl and Lisa together at the Hayes estate in upstate New York. They sat together under a grand old tree under star-filled skies, and Karl told her that he had been reassigned to Base Sara, a scientific observation post on Mars. He had pointed out the planet and confessed how torn he was to be leaving her. But there was no place on Earth for him any longer; even the Robotech project had been co-opted by the militaristic power wing of the Alliance. Instead of profiting from the miraculous find, they were merely gearing up for an anticipated war, a *projected* war.

She knew it was the right move for him, even if it was the wrong move for *them*. But that night her young mind had seized on a plan she hoped would keep them together: She would enlist in the Defense Force and would apply for an assignment to Sara Base.

She had confessed her love for Karl.

And lost him to the stars.

But she made good her promise, and with her father's assistance had received a security clearance and an assignment to Macross Island to work under Dr. Lang aboard the SDF-1.

She and Karl never saw each other again. But there were letters and tapes and the occasional transworld calls. Karl was in his element there, and all signs had pointed to her being able to join him soon. Until war had reached out its long arm and seized on the one place humankind had yet to spill blood. Sara Base became a graveyard overnight, almost a symbol of humankind's need to take war with it wherever it set foot in the universe.

The SDF-1 became her future from that moment on. She had thrown herself into the project with a fever born of forgetting that meant for rapid advancement but left little time for personal growth. Vanessa and Claudia chided her for her attachment to the ship, and sometimes she knew that she did come across as cold and distant.

The old sourpuss!

It was left unfinished between her and Karl, as if emotional time had been frozen on the night she learned about Base Sara's destruction.

This planetary touchdown then was more than a mere landing to her; it was an emotional pilgrimage. Karl

Riber was alive in her heart, moment to moment; to her it meant that he could really be alive, one of a group of survivors here. He had said to her, *We'll be together again someday, when the Earth is at peace*. Love was simply not meant to perish in angry flames; love couldn't be extinguished by war!

Gloval was shouting her name; she turned a confused face toward him, caught between past and future in a present that was of her own making.

"Lisa, what's wrong? Are you sure you're feeling all right?"

She composed herself and awaited his command.

"Send out a Cat's-Eye recon unit. Order them to report any anomalies in their findings—any at all."

Lisa turned to her task. *Let him be alive*, she prayed to herself.

The Cat's-Eye recon scanned the deserted base and radioed its findings to the bridge of the SDF-1: no sign of the enemy, no sign of life of any kind. And yet, inexplicably, data continued to pour into the onboard computers. Somehow one of the Sara Base computers had gone online. Captain Gloval was convinced of this much. Still, wary of a possible enemy trap, he convened a special meeting with colonels Maistroff and Caruthers and high-ranking officials of Macross City to discuss the prospect of setting the giant space fortress down on the surface of Mars.

There were two reasons for attempting such a landing, as opposed to holding the fortress in low orbit and using cargo ships and drones to ferry up the much-needed supplies. The primary reason was that a setdown would enable ground crews to repair damage sustained during four months of space warfare. Most of these re-

pairs could not be effected in deep space or even in low
orbit without the constant threat of enemy sneak attacks
and the overwhelming logistical problems that extended
extravehicular activity would entail. The second advantage, although less clear-cut, was of greater concern to
Gloval and Lang than to the Macross City leaders, for
whom replenished supplies was reason enough. The fact
was that the SDF-1 *had never been landed*; the closest it
had come was more a controlled drop than an actual
landing, months ago when the antigravity devices had
torn through the hull of the ship and it had fallen back to
its docking bay supports on Macross Island. The lower
gravity on Mars would allow engineering to stage a dress
rehearsal of the landing they would have to perform once
the fortress reached Earth.

Recalling that first day of attack, Gloval resisted an
urge to dwell on how defenseless he had felt with the
ship grounded. There was no assurance that this
wouldn't be the case again, but he had to convince himself that the advantages outweighed the risks.

It took two days to bring the SDF-1 down.

Astrogation held her in stationary orbit for what
seemed an eternity, and then the fortress was allowed to
begin its slow nerve-racking descent to the surface of
Mars. Gloval sat at the helm wondering what surprise
Lang's half grasp on Robotechnology might result in this
time, but to his relief and to the delight of everyone onboard, the SDF-1 was set down without incident. After
months in space it was difficult to believe they were
down on solid ground once again. It made no difference
that this wasn't their homeworld; after all, humankind
had once occupied this planet, and that was reason
enough to call it home for the moment.

Half of Macross City jammed itself onto the observa-

tion deck after the all-clear was sounded and the ship
had docked. At least half that number would have gladly
disembarked then and there to begin new lives for themselves; but there would be no liberty for civilians at this
port.

Gloval continued to have misgivings—he felt as if he
was standing on solid ground with nothing beneath his
feet. For this reason he ordered the ship down at a point
several kilometers from Sara Base. Destroids were then
deployed to secure a supply route, with squadrons of
Veritech fighters launched to provide cover. The Cat's-
Eye recon plane continued its sweeps over the area, and
long-range radar watched the skies. When Gloval was
convinced that there was no threat to their position or
operation, he ordered that the ship be moved closer to
the base, employing the auxiliary lifters and gravity control system, something they wouldn't have been able to
do on Earth.

Now the base complex, what remained of it, lay
spread out below the ship. From the bridge, the crew
could observe the destruction that had been visited upon
it, a grim reminder of the days when humankind was at
war with itself. It was a forlorn-looking place covered
with debris swept in by the continuous Martian winds.

The supply routes secure, Battloids began their patrol, gatling weapons ready. A long line of wheeled and
treaded transport vehicles now stretched from the loading bays of the *Daedalus* and the *Prometheus* to the
heart of Sara.

Lisa was waiting for the right moment; if she didn't
act quickly, though, there wouldn't be another chance.
Data from the base was still coming in, and Gloval had
yet to organize a recon team to investigate the source of

the transmissions. Finally she gathered up enough nerve and turned to the captain.

"Requesting your permission to leave the ship, sir, and recon the interior of the base."

The captain regarded her with concern. "But Lisa—"

She interrupted him. "I'd like to check out the source of those signals, sir. There could be survivors here!" Only when she caught the look of protective paternalism in his eyes did she break down. "Please, sir. It's important to me." She had no idea whether Gloval knew anything about her past; but he knew her as a crewmember, knew when she needed his attention.

Claudia offered an unsolicited assist. "I'll cover her duties here," she told the captain.

Gloval thought it over. Anyone who was within 500 kilometers of the base would have already come running. But there was something so personal in her insistence that he decided to allow her to go.

"But I want you to take two security personnel with you!" he called out as she hurried from the bridge.

Lisa ignored the captain's command; after all, it hadn't been issued as a direct order. She outfitted herself with helmet and environment suit, radio, and laser side-arm and took charge of a small personnel carrier from supply.

Had she been thinking about it, she might have compared her short ride across the Martian wastes to the driving training she'd undergone on the moon years ago, but her thoughts were elsewhere. She had to find Karl and renew their life together or discover for herself that he was dead.

The base had the familiar look and feel of the countless war-torn cities she'd experienced on Earth—not voluntarily abandoned but simply cut down in its prime. All life had been sucked from the place in an instant, and that sort of ending always left ghosts lingering about. She could sense their presence all around her, almost as if they were still confused by what had occurred here and were now demanding an explanation from this stranger who was visiting their resting place. Yes, it was like those ravaged cities but more so: The howling of the winds was louder and angrier, the soil appeared more blood-stained, and there was never a blue sky here.

She used the homing device to direct her to the source of the transmissions received by the SDF-1. They emanated from a large building, central to the complex, that had served as the communications center. She entered this through the blown front hatchway and made her way through deserted halls to the computer room, the sound of her own breathing heavy in her ears. Everywhere she looked there was evidence of the disaster. The scientists who were stationed here must have had some sort of warning, though, because there were no bodies lying about—how she had feared that!—just general disarray, as if there had been a last-minute effort to collect what they could and leave this place before the sky fell.

At last she reached computer control. She stood motionless in the doorway and peered into the deserted room: chairs tipped over, papers strewn about, a carpet of glass shards from blown monitor screens wall-to-wall. But at the far end of the room there were flashing console lights, greens and reds, and an on-line computer frantically emptying its memory banks across a monitor screen no eyes were meant to read, like an infant left crying in a crib. Lisa walked over to the machine and shut it down. She turned and took another look around the room, puzzling over its emptiness.

So there was no half-starved band of survivors huddled in one sealed room using the computer as shipwrecked sailors would a signal fire. Just a machine that had somehow activated itself.

The way memories did.

Hidden in a deep chasm fifteen kilometers from Sara Base, Khyron and his attack force of 200 Battlepods waited. The Backstabber himself occupied his Officer's Pod, a mecha different from the rest, with lasers protruding like whiskers from its elongated snout and two arms that were deadly cannons. He ingested the dried and intoxicating leaves of the Invid Flower while monitoring reports from his squad leaders who were holding at other points along the perimeter.

A Micronian recon ship had already overflown the canyon and failed to detect the presence of his troops. The abandoned base was surrounded, the gravity mines were in place, and the fortress had set down just where he had predicted it would. The foolish Micronians had taken the bait—an on-line computer—and the trap was almost ready to be sprung. Soon he would capture Zor's ship, *for the glory of the Zentraedi*! And for the honor of Khyron. It would be a shame if he was forced to take on the fortress himself. He did *so* want the credit to go to Breetai. If only things weren't going so slowly. The leaves always made him somewhat impatient.

"Gerao, aren't those gravity mines ready yet?" he shouted into his comlink mike.

The Battlepod speaker crackled with static and the monitor erupted into patternless noise bars before

Gerao's face appeared on the screen. His droid team was operating at almost three kilometers below the surface. Gerao may have won the collision bet, but it didn't pay to best one's commander. Khyron laughed to himself.

"The energy accumulation is up to seventy percent, my lord. Not much longer."

"Blast it, this waiting is irritating me! Drive those droids harder, Gerao, or I'll leave you buried on this godforsaken world. You have my word on it!"

Gerao's emphatic salute signaled that he understood Khyron's threat completely. He signed off. Khyron began to drum his fingers on the console. *Zor's ship*, he thought to himself. Why was Commander in Chief Dolza wasting his time with this one when there were countless worlds left to conquer? Since when were the Zentraedi errand boys? If the Robotech Masters were so desperate about getting Zor's Protoculture matrix back, they could go retrieve it themselves. What did Khyron care about Protoculture? It was the Invid Flowers that were important to him . . . He picked up one of the dried petals and regarded it lovingly: Here was the true power.

As Khyron was placing the petal in his mouth, the face of one of his troops surfaced on the Officer's Pod commo screen.

"We've waited long enough, Commander," the soldier said. "I'm going in now. Any longer and we will jeopardize our mission."

To Khyron's amazement, the soldier's Battlepod fired its thrusters and began to lift off from the chasm floor. Was he seeing things or had this fool actually decided to use his own initiative? Khyron was as fond of insolence as anyone, but this was pushing things too far. He allowed the pod to climb almost to the rim of the chasm before bringing up one of the cannon arms of his mecha and firing. The Battlepod took a direct hit, turned end over end, and plummeted and crashed on the chasm floor.

The pilots of two other pods hopped their crafts over to their fallen comrade and checked his status.

"He's still alive, my lord."

"So much the worse for him, then," yelled Khyron. "If I can wait here patiently, so can the rest of you. The next one who disobeys my orders will meet a worse fate. I promise you that!"

Khyron was imagining his underlings stiffening into postures of salute inside the pods when the voice of Gerao entered the headset.

"My lord, I fear that use of the cannon may have compromised our position. The Micronian recon plane is circling back in this direction."

"The recon plane! Gerao, are you ready with the mines?"

"Just ten percent more to go."

Khyron slapped his hands down on the pod console. "Ninety percent will have to be good enough. You have my permission to attack!"

Claudia was worried: There had been no word from Lisa for almost an hour now. The incoming data from the base had terminated, but the seismic sensors were picking up something new. Captain Gloval and Vanessa were trying to make sense of the readings.

"Nearby in the mountains, I think—a disturbance or explosion," said Vanessa.

"A landslide, perhaps."

"No, there's too much sonic attached to it. It must have been an explosion."

Gloval turned to Claudia. "Instruct the Cat's-Eye to make another pass over the eleven o'clock zone at the fifteen-kilometer perimeter. And see to it that recon readings are patched into the main screen here."

Claudia contacted the Cat's-Eye, and within minutes new data was filling the screen: The sensors indicated hundreds of individual mecha units moving in from the cavernous mountains that surrounded Sara Base.

"Battlepods!" said Gloval. He ordered Claudia to sound general quarters. "Recall all transport vehicles immediately and scramble the Veritech fighters! They won't catch us napping this time!" Gloval paced the bridge, then threw himself into the command chair. "Activate the gravity control system and prepare the ship for takeoff."

Claudia swung around from her terminal. "But Captain, Lisa's still out there. She'll never make it back in time."

Gloval waved his hand in a gesture of dismissal. "I told her I didn't want her to enter that base. Now she'll have to come up in one of the VTs."

Claudia hid a look of concern from Gloval and carried out her orders. But something was wrong: The ship wasn't lifting off. The gravity control system wasn't damaged, there were correct readings on all the sensors, but the SDF-1 would not rise. It bellowed and shuddered like some captured beast.

"Captain," Vanessa managed to shout above the noise, "the seismic sensor indicates an intense gravity field underlying the base!"

Gloval leaped from his seat to study the threat board.

"Gravity mines! So this is what the enemy has in mind—they mean to pin us down like a trapped insect. Shut down all engines before she comes apart at the seams!"

"Battlepods!" said Claudia.

Gloval and the bridge crew turned to face the front bays: The Martian sky was filled with enemy mecha.

CHAPTER SIX

It's become my routine these past two months to wander over to the observation dome and spend hours at the scope watching our beautiful blue and white world transit the Martian night. How bright, how incredibly alive and tranquil, Earth appears from afar! And how misleading that impression is . . . I often think about our last night together. It was more difficult for me to leave you than to leave our planet, the global madness, the small minds at work who have robbed us of our dreams. But I don't want to get started on all this again; I want to talk about this place, and how happy I know you will be here. The stars seem close enough to touch, our distant sun no less warm, and even these incessant winds do not disturb . . . Base Sara is a new experiment in peace, a new experiment in the future . . .

Karl Riber, *Collected Letters*

THE BATTLEPODS AND CARAPACE FIGHTERS OF THE Botoru Seventh left the cover of the mountain chasms and descended on Sara Base. Khyron led the assault, screaming into his communicator, "Kill them, kill them all!"

The Robotech forces threw everything they had into the Martian sky. Battloids and Spartan defenders took up positions on the base, while squadrons of Veritechs went up to meet the enemy one on one. The main batteries and CIWS Phalanx guns of the grounded space fortress rotated into position and filled the thin air with orange tracers, armor-piercing discarding sabot rounds, and deadly thunder.

In an attempt to cut off the supply line to the SDF-1, Khyron and his forces went after the transports first. The pods fell from the Martian sky unleashing a torrent of energy bolts and missiles. The all-terrain trucks bounded off the gravel highway to evade fire, but scarcely a dozen made it to the fortress intact. Explosions tossed the vehicles off the ground like toys, and soon there was only a pathway of fire where the vehicles had once traveled.

The Destroids were next on Khyron's list; then he turned his attention to the Battleloids and Guardians.

The Battloids of the Skull Team were positioned along the SDF-1's defensive perimeter when they received launch orders. Roy and Rick transformed their mecha to Guardian mode and lifted off from blasting carpets to engage the enemy.

Rick retracted the legs and threw the fighter into a long vertical climb, exchanging fire with three pods on the way up. The three gave chase while he banked at the crest of his ascent and dropped off into a fusillade fall, weapons blazing as he came back down on them. Heat-seekers ripped from his mecha, scoring hits against two pods.

Rick and the remaining enemy raced above the rough terrain, trading shots. At the foot of the mountains they split apart, only to encounter each other at the craggy summits. It was a game of aerial chicken, pod and fighter on a collision course, Zentraedi and Terran pilots emptying their guns.

Rick yo-yoed and took the fight deeper into the mountains. The enemy pursued him, launching rockets which Rick's mecha successfully evaded with breaks and jinks and high barrel rolls.

Skull twenty-three banked sharply now and fell away into a narrow valley, luring its opponent toward a forest of wind-eroded rock spires. Rick used two of his rockets to blast an opening for himself and dove in. The pod stayed with him but was having trouble negotiating the forest's tight groupings of columns. Too late, the enemy pilot attempted to pull out; one of the pod's clawlike legs snagged on a spire, and the pod suddenly became a high-speed pinball, careening from tower to tower. Flames and debris from the resounding explosion tore past Rick's mecha as he climbed from the canyon.

This was more like it, he told himself, rejoining his battle group on the Martian plain. Sky above, ground below. Sound and light, explosions of finality. No clouds for cover, but it seemed as though you could see forever through the thin air.

Just then Roy's face appeared on the left screen of his cockpit.

"What d' ya think, Little Brother? It's a little like the old days, isn't it?"

"The 'old' days, yeah, *four months ago!*"

Roy laughed. "Let's get 'em, tiger!"

Rick watched his friend's fighter face down two of the pods and dispatch both of them. He quickly scanned the busy sky: If each Veritech could take out two pods, the enemy would only have them outnumbered four to one.

From the bridge of the SDF-1, Gloval and his crew had a clear view of the ongoing massacre. Brilliant strobe-like flashes of explosive light spilled in through the forward and side bays as the enemy continued to pour fire at the ship. The fortress rocked and vibrated to the staccato beat of battle. The Martian landscape had become an inferno.

"The sixth and eighth Spartan divisions have been wiped out, Captain," Claudia reported. "Veritech squadrons are sustaining heavy casualties."

Gloval paced the deck, fingers of one hand tugging at his thick mustache. "There must be a way out of this . . ." He turned to Vanessa. "Put the seismic schematic on the screen again."

Gloval studied the computer graphic display as it came up. The source of the induced gravitation that held the ship captive was located some three kilometers beneath the surface. Gloval now had Kim project a schematic of the underground power center that fueled Sara Base. He stepped back to take in both screens, folded his arms across his chest, and nodded.

"It's just as I thought. There is a reflex furnace beneath Sara." Reflex power was one of Robotechnology's first by-products—back in more peaceful times. "If we were to overload it, the explosion that would result might take out the enemy's gravity mines as well."

Gloval instructed Vanessa to run a computer simulation based on the available data. Then he turned to Claudia: "Contact Lisa, immediately."

Lisa was trying to figure a way out of Sara Base when Gloval's call came through. With what she recalled from her engineering courses and the technical assists the SDF-1 onboard computers would provide, there was a good chance that she'd be able to shut down the reflex furnace as Gloval requested. He instructed her to keep her radio tuned in to the bridge frequency so that they could monitor her location and position.

The first step would be to get herself safely from the

communications center to the main power station, which meant an unescorted trip through the thick of the fighting. There was one other option, though, and it would require her to be out in the open only for a short time. The power center was linked to the barracks building through a system of underground tunnels and access corridors. And the barracks was just a short hop through hell.

Lisa poised herself on the threshold of the communication building's blown hatch. Ground-shaking explosions were going off all around her. Alien pods, hopping nimbly through the devastation, were leveling everything in sight. Hundreds of missiles corkscrewed overhead, converging on what was left of the supply line and the fortress itself. Lisa's dream was finished, and Sara Base was finished with it. She pushed herself from the front entry like a parachutist leaving an old-style aircraft and flung herself into the firestorm. She ran a slalom course, jagging left and right through fields of fire, and made it to the safety of the barracks just short of a violent blast that took out the area she'd left behind. The concussion threw her off her feet, but she was unhurt.

Inside, she accessed information from the SDF-1 to locate the main shaft elevators. There was auxiliary power here, so she would be able to ride down to the underground room.

The descent was a long one. It felt as though she were traveling into the very bowels of the fiery planet. Each level lessened the effects of the overhead bombardment until the world seemed silent once again.

Stepping out at Sublevel Fifteen, she made her way to the control room. There was an uncommon, low-level vibration down here, and she was forced to move with more exertion, almost as though she'd been returned to

Earth gravity. She reasoned that the enemy gravity mines were responsible for this.

It took Lisa several minutes to locate the furnace controls, a confusing array of switches, dials, and meters, antiquated and needlessly complex. There were redundant systems and far too many command switches and manually operated crossovers. But instructions from the onboard computer simplified her task. Finally she had the reflex computers programmed for overload. The control systems that allowed excess charge buildup to be safely shunted into runoffs were now damped down, and all backup outlets were similarly closed. Next she instructed the CPUs that operated the furnace to bring the power up to maximum, canceling out the safety programs with override commands.

Warning lights were starting to flash on the console, and she thought she could detect the sound of warning sirens and klaxons going off somewhere. The sequence, however, had kicked in several other built-in safety systems that were unanticipated: Hatchways were beginning to lower throughout the room. According to an overhead digital clock, she had less than fifteen minutes to get off the base.

Lisa returned to the main elevator and rode the car back to ground level. The sounds of battle had increased. She tried to retrace her path to the entrance, but the barracks had taken several hits, and debris now blocked the corridor. There was an unobstructed second corridor that led to the officers' quarters; a hatchway there would allow her to exit on the other side of the building. She entered this and was making for the hatch, when the corridor suddenly sealed itself off. Iron doors dropped from overhead vaults at both ends, trapping her inside.

Hatchways to individual quarters lined both sides of

the corridor, and while she was opening each of these looking for some way out, a terrible thought occurred to her: What if one of these rooms had belonged to Karl?

In the dim light, Lisa's fingers traced the letters of raised name tags on the doors, and it wasn't long before she found RIBER, KARL.

Slowly the will to survive began to abandon her. All she could feel now was a terrible sadness and a pain from long ago, as though her body was recalling the hurt and bringing it up to the surface.

She hit the button that opened the hatchway to Karl's quarters and stood at the threshold, afraid to enter, supporting herself against the doorjamb. "Oh, Karl," she said to whatever ghosts were lurking there.

Lisa entered, mindless of the countdown to self-destruction.

"The destruct sequence has been initiated, Captain," Claudia said. "T minus ten minutes and counting."

Gloval nodded his head in approval. "Good. I knew Lisa could do it. Now, issue a recall order to our remaining Destroids and Valkyries. But I want them to pull back slowly. With a little luck we'll catch the enemy in *our* trap this time."

"Nine minutes and counting, Captain."

"Contact Lisa; let's see how she's making out."

Claudia tried, but there was no response. The radio transmitter was still on, but Lisa wasn't answering the call.

"Lisa, come in, please," Claudia said. "She's not responding, Captain."

Gloval rose from his chair. "If she's still on-line, we should be able to get a fix on her position."

Kim already had it up on the screen.

"She's in Barracks C. But she's not moving."

"She could be hurt, or trapped," said Gloval. "Claudia, quickly, contact the Skull Leader."

Rick released two rockets and dove under the Battlepods. White-hot shrapnel impacted against his fighter, and the shock wave threw him into an involuntary sink.

He narrowly missed buying it at the hands of an enemy Officer's Pod that leaped into view out of nowhere. It was the same one he had seen on and off throughout the battle. And whoever piloted it was someone to fear. Rick had seen the pod take out three Veritechs in one pass, and later he had seen that same pilot blow away two of his own men to get to one of the Robotech Valkyries.

Roy pulled alongside Rick, gesturing to the enemy mecha. His face was on twenty-three's left screen.

"You wanna watch that one, Rick. He means business."

"Let's gang up on him, buddy."

"Negative, Rick. We've got new orders. Seems that Commander Hayes has gotten herself stranded on the base and it's up to us to rescue her."

"Hey, like we don't have more pressing matters at hand?"

"Come on, I thought that damsels in distress were your stock 'n' trade, Little Brother."

"One damsel at a time, Roy. One at a time."

Roy's face became serious. "Patch your system into the SDF-1 mainboard and home in on the signal they transmit. I'll be covering you."

"Roger," Rick said. "One rescue coming up."

He pushed the fighter into a shallow dive that brought him into and through a group of alien pods. Those that didn't take each other out in an effort to bring him down, Rick dispatched with close-in laser fire directed at the pods' fuel lines. Roy was running interference up ahead, diverting some of the pods positioned between Rick and the base.

Rick dropped the fighter to ground level, relaxed back into his seat, lowering his mind into transitional alpha and directing the Veritech's transformation to Guardian mode. The fighter was soon tearing along the ground in a sort of combat crouch, gatling cannon held out front by the huge grappling hands of the mecha. Rick rode out a cluster of explosions in this form, then hit his thrusters and brought the mecha into full Battloid mode to deal with several pods along his projected course.

Upright, the Battloid swung the cannon in an arc and trap-shot two of the pods. A half twist and Rick beat another to the draw.

Rick let Roy deal out justice to the rest and shifted his attention to the homing signal. Info from the SDF-1 bridge told him precisely where the commander was located: inside the barracks building, just on the other side of the wall in front of him.

In four minutes the entire base was going to be a memory. And that didn't leave him enough time to use the doorway. He retransformed to Guardian mode and readied the massive metalshod fists of the mecha.

Now it was Lisa's turn to play the ghost.

She had walked through Riber's quarters, insulated from the harsh atmosphere by her suit, arms extended, gloved fingers reaching out and touching everything in the small room, expectant, in search of something she couldn't identify or name. What was it she hoped to find here? she asked herself. It was as if Karl's clothes, still in the wardrobe closet, his bed, reading light, and phone held clues to some mystery she hoped to unravel.

And now as she sat at his desk, paging through his notebooks and reading the titles of the books stacked there—*The Martian Cronicles*, *Mankind Evolving*, *Gandhi's Truth*—Lisa realized that she would never get over his loss; she would never be able to leave this place. Her life, along with Riber's, had ended here six years ago.

She fell forward onto the open notebooks and began to weep. Claudia was desperately calling to her through the headset, but Lisa already felt disconnected from that present. She switched off the radio transmitter. She was about to raise the faceshield of her helmet when she heard her name called out through a speaker phone of some sort.

On the other side of the room's thick translucent window. she could discern the shape of a Veritech fighter—a veiled Guardian behind a Permaglass gate.

"Commander Hayes," the voice called out. "Please stand back. I'm going to crash my way in."

Quickly, she switched her radio back on.

"Whoever you are, stay away from here. Return to the ship. That's an order."

The fighter pilot paid her no mind.

"Stand back. My orders are to get you out of here."

Before she could speak again, the Guardian's huge hand had smashed through the window and the pilot— Rick Hunter! —was staring at her from the cockpit.

"Climb aboard—quickly! We don't have much time left!"

"I'm not leaving this room!"

"One minute and counting, Commander."

"I don't care! Go on, do you hear me, save yourself!"

She saw him shake his head.

"I don't know what's going on here, but you're coming with me."

And in an instant Lisa was held fast in the grip of the Guardian's hand. It was useless to struggle; the Veritech was already backing away from the barracks building and preparing for takeoff.

She found herself reaching out toward Riber's room nevertheless, clinging to it with all the strength she could summon, screaming out his name as the fighter launched itself and sped from the burning base.

Khyron pressed the attack, urging his forces onward with calls to glory and promises of promotion; when those failed, he resorted to simple threats and imprecations. Several times during the exercise he had decided to deal out punishments on the spot, and occasionally he had been forced to sacrifice the innocent. But this was all part of the warrior's life, not regrettable but expected behavior.

It had been a glorious battle—up until now.

The Micronians had begun to retreat toward Zor's ship, a retreat with at least three-quarters of their original forces still occupying the arena. He was confused and angered. Were the Micronians such spineless creatures that they would choose surrender over death in battle? Zor's ship, held fast by the gravity mines, wasn't going anywhere, so what did these fools expect to gain by a retreat? It would only mean a nastier mop-up operation for Khyron's troops. The space fortress would have to be stormed, or perhaps he would decide to starve them out; but in either case the end result would be death, so why not go out fighting?

Gerao was reporting certain anomalies in the gravity

mine field—some sort of pressure buildup the sensors had yet to identify—but with the Micronians on the run, this was hardly the moment for caution or indecisiveness. Khyron would have the enemy captain's head before nightfall!

The Zentraedi forces had routed the enemy from the base, and their commander was about to join them there, when the surface of the planet began to quake with unnatural force. Some massive explosion deep below ground level was working its way upward. And when it broke the planet's skin, it was greater than anyone—Zentraedi or Earthling—might have expected.

In an instant, the base and most of Khyron's occupying army were obliterated as a tower of raw unleashed energy shot from within the planet. Through the blinding glow of the initial explosion, Khyron could see Zor's ship lifting off, just moments before a second explosion of equivalent force atomized what was left of the area.

Khyron's Officer's Pod was far enough away to withstand the blast, heat, and follow-up shock waves and firestorms.

Madness, Khyron thought. *Madness*!

He raised the cockpit shield of the Battlepod and sat for a moment in stunned silence. Thick clouds of rust-colored dust were being sucked into the area. Zor's ship was just a preternatural shimmer in the Martian sky. The Micronians had surprised him.

Unpredictability was something to fear and respect in an opponent. But failure in battle was something that could not be tolerated.

He vented his anger by smashing his fists into the console of the Battlepod, then collapsed back into the seat, spent. He reached out for the dried leaves of the

Flower of Life, ingesting several of these and urging their narcotic effect to wash over him. Ultimately Khyron smiled maliciously. He gazed up at the dwindling space fortress and said aloud:

"We'll meet again, Micronians. And next time I will give you no quarter."

CHAPTER
SEVEN

I admit it: In those early days I had trouble playing by the rules. Of course, ultimately I learned to return salutes, use the proper phrases, demonstrate respect for my superior officers, and generally behave like a model Robotech soldier. But I continued to have real problems with the system of promotion. If it had been up to me, medals would have been handed out to everyone who went out there. There wasn't one among us who wasn't deserving; not one among us who wasn't qualified to lead.

The Collected Journals of Admiral Rick Hunter

THERE WAS A SPECIAL DATA CHAMBER IN BREETAI'S flagship that was off limits to all but the highest-ranking officers of the Zentraedi elite. In here were stored the historical records of the Zentraedi race: documentation of past victories, military campaigns, great moments in the lives of great warrior leaders. In addition to these were banks of information relating to the Invid and several dozen other sentient life forms that inhabited the Fourth Quadrant of the galactic local group. As chief science officer and transcultural adviser on all issues dealing with interracial contact (more frequently, conquest), it was Exedore's duty to commit to memory a vast amount of this accumulated lore and knowledge. Indeed, this room belonged more to the misshapen Zentraedi than to any other. And the more he delved into data pertaining to the Micronians, the more apprehensive he became. The pursuit of Zor's ship, and this continued contact with the ship's Micronian warriors, was destined to end in unprecedented failure—an undoing of all that had been carefully laid down and preserved for millennia. Try as he might, Exedore could not put this thought from his mind. If the Zentraedi were defeated, what then could stand in the way of the dreaded *Invid*?

He had mentioned these misgivings to Breetai, careful to couch his phrases in such a way that no fear or cowardice could be inferred; he had even gone so far as to quote some of the documents to the commander, pointing out the specific warnings about contact with the Micronians. Legends which spoke of a Micronian secret weapon that would be used against any invading race. But his words fell on deaf ears. Breetai was, after all, a military tactician; like most of his race he lived and breathed for battle and warfare—the Zentraedi were born to this. Moreover there was some unspoken fascination at work here, as if in some half-understood way Breetai too was aware of Exedore's thoughts about destiny and undoing.

Just now the two Zentraedi were standing together in the observation bubble of the bridge. The SDF-1, in high relief against a starlit crescent of this system's fourth planet, filled the forward screen. Khyron's forces, though unsuccessful in capturing the ship when it had been lured into Breetai's trap, had nonetheless prevented the Micronians from gaining any distance to their homeworld.

"It amazes me that they have managed to come this far," said Breetai.

"Yes, Commander, and they will fight more fiercely as they near their planet. I fear that the ship itself may be destroyed long before we can enforce a surrender."

Breetai became agitated. "That must not be allowed to happen, Exedore. My orders have been most specific: I want the fortress captured intact and undamaged. The *ship* is our primary concern, not the people in it."

"Sir, I fear that Khyron understands destruction only. 'Capture' is too subtle a strategy for him to comprehend."

Breetai shot his adviser a look. "Khyron is a Zentraedi. He'll do as he's ordered or face the consequences."

Exedore bowed slightly. "Certainly, my lord."

Would that it were so, he thought. And did the Micronian commander in charge of Zor's ship have similar issues to deal with, or were orders carried out without question at all times? Like the Zentraedi, the Micronians were a warlike race; but had they too arrived at that evolutionary point where individual initiative was willingly relinquished for the greater glory of the whole? The data documents were not clear on this point.

Exedore stared at the fortress, as if attempting to project himself onboard. What were the Micronians planning? he wondered. What would any *one* member of that race be thinking at this very moment?

She loves clothes. Her favorite colors are shades of pink and purple. She lacquers each fingernail with a different color polish. She likes to wear dangling, outrageous earrings, shoes that give her more height and match her mood, bright belts with large buckles... "It's no use!" Rick said out loud. He got up off the bed and began to pace the scant distance it took to cover his new quarters wall to wall.

The invitation to Minmei's birthday party lay unopened on his bed, the envelope sealed with a paste-on red velvet heart. *Cute*. There was no need to read it—half of his division had received invitations, and everyone was flashing them in front of his face with knowing smiles. He wasn't sure that he was even interested in going to the party under the circumstances. When it was just the two of them, everything was fine. But in a large group, Minmei wanted center stage and Rick often felt like just another nobody in the audience. Just another faceless member of Minmei's adoring public. *Neglected*. Yeah, that was how he felt. And jealous, he had to admit it. Angry, confused, depressed . . . the list went on and on. It was almost as long as the list of possible gifts he'd formulated. But none of the items seemed quite right, not one of them was *perfect*, and that was what he was shooting for. Something that would say what he couldn't confess.

And just what was that? he asked himself. He wanted to tell her how special she was—how beautiful, and sexy, and charming. How flirtatious and conceited and spoiled and—

All this was getting him nowhere—fast. He collapsed onto the bed, put his hands under his head, and stared at the ceiling. When he closed his eyes and tried to think things through once more, something unexpected happened: The face of Lisa Hayes filled his mind. This wasn't something new, but it continued to take him by surprise. The truth was, it had been happening a lot since Sara Base.

Was he really such an idiot that he was going to invite

yet another woman to run roughshod over him? An older woman at that, a superior officer who gave every indication of despising him in spite of his rescue efforts on her behalf? A cold and distant plain-looking woman who seemed more a part of the SDF-1 than a part of the crew? So why was he suddenly feeling that she too needed protection and affection?—*his* protection, *his* affection. But Lisa occupied a different place in his heart than Minmei, someplace he couldn't reach with thoughts alone.

Rick was rescued from this by a call announced through the intrabarracks comm system.

"Attention the following personnel: report to headquarters: third lieutenants Justin Black and James Ralton; second lieutenants Xian Lu, Carroll James, and Marcus Miller; first lieutenants Thomas Lawson and Adam Olsen..."

Rick listened for a moment, lost interest, and was about to rehash his dilemma, when he heard his own name called.

He made himself presentable and left the barracks, walking listlessly toward headquarters and wondering just what he might have done to get himself called on the carpet this time. He ran through a mental list of the possibilities as he rode the elevator to the command level of the ship.

It was a day for lists, that was for sure.

A female lieutenant led him into a briefing room where the others whose names had been called were already gathered. Rick fell into an end position and looked down the line: Black, Ralton, Olsen...these guys were all square shooters. No one needed to read them the riot act, and not one of them seemed the slightest bit concerned; just the opposite, in fact: confidence and pride radiated from each face.

When a captain called attention, Rick squared his shoulders and feigned unconcern. Colonel Maistroff and some of the top brass entered the room. The colonel seated himself at a long table and glanced through the files piled in front of him; then he cleared his throat and addressed the line.

"Since the battle for Sara Base on Mars, the men assembled here have established for themselves records of bravery under fire. Therefore, I am pleased to award them the titanium Medal of Valor for their distinguished service. Gentlemen: We proudly acknowledge your achievements!"

The female lieutenant had carried over a flat unlidded box, and from this Maistroff lifted out the medals, pinning one to each breast in the line and offering his hand in congratulations. Rick wanted to pinch himself to make certain he wasn't dreaming. He craned his neck to try to get a good look at the medal after Maistroff had decorated him.

When the brief ceremony ended, Rick left the room. He found Roy Fokker waiting for him, all smiles and beaming like a proud older brother.

"Nice going, Rick."

They shook hands and embraced. Rick said, "I still can't believe it."

"Amateur civilian ace for eight years running and you're not used to awards by now?" Roy laughed. "Come on down to my office for a minute."

They caught up on the events of the past few days as they walked. At the office, Roy motioned Rick to a chair and positioned himself behind the desk opposite him. He opened a drawer, retrieved something, and tossed it to Rick.

It was a small, flat leather case. Rick hefted it and asked, "What is it?"

Roy's smile was enigmatic. "Go on, open it."

Rick snapped open the lid: Lieutenant's bars rested on green velvet beds.

"You've been promoted, Rick."

Lieutenant Rick Hunter.

Rick asked Roy to say it so he could get used to the sound of it.

"Lieutenant Rick Hunter."

Rick signaled his approval with a nod. It sounded fine. Next he turned his attention to the information contained in the dossiers Roy had given him.

I'm assigning two subordinates to your command.

Some of the dossier material flashed across the monitor screen on Roy's desk: CORPORAL BEN DIXON; 378 HOURS IN FLIGHT SIMULATION AND 66 ACTUAL HOURS. CLASS A. MAXIMILLIAN STERLING; 320 HOURS IN FLIGHT SIMULATION AND 50 ACTUAL HOURS. CLASS A.

While he listened, Rick absently fingered the medal of valor pinned to his jacket.

"These guys are novices, Roy."

Roy stuck out his jaw. "You're the old veteran now?"

"Well, I've flown more missions than these two."

"To me you're not a lot different from them, Little Brother. You've flown more than some but a lot less than most of us. It's too early for you to get cocky."

Rick considered this sullenly. He removed the medal and regarded it. *What is it really? Just something to*

*make me feel better about going out as cannon fodder
again.*

Roy had gotten up to answer a knock at the door, and
when Rick looked up, he found his two new subordinates
stepping forward in formal salute to introduce themselves.

Dixon, the larger of the two by almost a foot, was
muscular and aggressive. He had a crop of undisciplined
brown hair that rose from his head like flames caught
in freeze frame. There was a note of arrogance about
him, but this was softened somewhat by his husky
self-mocking laughter. Sterling, in contrast, was mild-
mannered and soft of voice. And yet there was something almost false about his humility. He wore his hair
long, with uneven bangs that kept falling in front of his
aviator glasses. It was unusual to meet a pilot with im-
paired vision, and Rick reasoned that Sterling's talents
had to outweigh the disadvantages presented by less-
than-perfect eyesight.

Rick acknowledged their salutes, and Roy made the
informal introductions. But after a few minutes of pleasantries, Rick was beginning to feel uncomfortable with
his two new dependents and took advantage of a lapse in
the conversation to excuse himself. Minmei's party
would be kicking off soon, and he wanted to catch her
alone for at least a few minutes. However, when Ben and
Max suddenly expressed an interest in accompanying
him, Rick reconsidered his options: Showing up at Minmei's with new lieutenant's bars *and* two subordinates in
tow would surely gain him some points. At least it would
show her that his superiors viewed him as responsible
and serious, even if she chose not to.

So the three of them left Fokker's together, already
exchanging stories and searching out common ground.

They tubed into Macross City, hitting a few spots on the way, and it wasn't long before they were fast friends.

Macross was a different experience each time Rick visited it. Resident old-timers—people born back in the 'forties and 'fifties—claimed that it would have taken generations to construct what Robotech engineers and crews managed in a week. All of this was due to technological advances brought about with the arrival of the SDF-1. Some of the city had been "created" through the use of Enhanced Video Emulation—the people were fed illusions as in some turn-of-the century film—but most of it was a real, pulsing metropolis now. Certainly no city on Earth could boast of a park with views to match those from Macross Central. You were not just staring up at the stars from the benches there; you were among them.

The three VT pilots were a few blocks from the White Dragon, when several "death-beds" rumbled by—huge flatbed vehicles carting off the battle-damaged remains of Veritech fighters to recycling. Without raw material, the SDF-1 techs had to reuse everything.

Rick looked over at his new comrades and studied their reaction to the passing wrecks. His jubilant mood had vanished. Fighter pilots were similarly recycled, he told himself.

"There's the whole truth about war," Rick said, gesturing to the death-beds.

"I don't want to end up like that," said Max.

Ben bellowed his laugh. "While I'm around you've got nothing to worry about."

Lieutenant Rick had an impromptu speech on the tip of his tongue, but he decided to let Dixon's remark slide. Ben would find out for himself soon enough.

The war machine would chew them up and spit them

out. You could only give it your best shot and hope the odds were in your favor.

"Luck" was a term the Zentraedi were unfamiliar with; their language contained no words for it, and their psychological makeup embraced no such concept.

Khyron had suffered a setback. It had nothing to do with chance or odds. He had failed because he had listened to Breetai and disregarded his own instincts. This would not happen again. This enemy was unpredictable. Where it would be advantageous to press an attack, they would retreat; where it would have been wise to use the massive firepower of Zor's ship, they instead relied on small fighters. And the worst of it was that they seemed to value life above all else. Sooner or later Khyron would have to play on that fear of death they carried around.

He had appointed a new second-in-command to replace Gerao, who was now in solitary confinement for having failed to detect the Micronians' countermeasures at the abandoned base. The blank faceplated visage of this second was currently on the monitor screen in Kyron's quarters.

"But, my lord," the second was saying, "what about Commander Breetai's reaction to our continued attacks? He has made it clear—"

"Forget about him! Do you dare question my authority?"

"My lord!" The second saluted.

"We'll deal with that ship in our own way. Now pay close attention: Breetai has prescribed war games for us. This is his way of humiliating me for our failures. But we're going to turn this opportunity to our advantage.

We're going to take that ship, if it takes every last piece of mecha in the Zentraedi armada!"

Things were quiet on the bridge of the SDF-1, a little too quiet to suit Claudia Grant. The ship had been in a deep-space orbit around Mars for scarcely a week, but that week felt like an eternity. And it had been that long since Lisa had exchanged more than three words with Claudia or any of the others on the bridge. Something had happened to Lisa down there, but even Claudia couldn't pry any of the details from her. To be sure, it had something to do with Karl Riber. Claudia figured that he must have been quite a man to keep Lisa in limbo for eight years. For most of the ship's crew and the population of Macross City the red planet afforded some sense of stability and center, but for Lisa it was a constant reminder of loss, an orbit of pain.

The enemy had been hammering away at them for the past week, determined to keep them from making any progress toward Earth. But the launch window for a return to Earth was still two weeks away, so they would have remained here regardless. Conserving fuel, making repairs, and using Mars's gravity to throw them toward Earth when the right moment came. Nevertheless, they had attempted to keep the planet between themselves and the enemy; until yesterday, when long-range recon units had reported that a sizable contingent of enemy ships had dropped to an inner orbit near the Martian moon Phobos. The enemy was sandwiching the fortress between their forces. Claudia was worried, and Lisa's continued silence and sulking were not helping at all.

Claudia held something in her hand she thought might break her friend's distracted mood: It was a dispatch from Maistroff's office listing the new field promotions.

Rick Hunter's name was on the list. Claudia tapped the dispatch against the palm of her left hand. Maybe anger was just what the doctor ordered.

She sidled over to Lisa, suppressing a grin as she handed over the dispatch.

Lisa accepted it disinterestedly and scanned the short column. Claudia watched her expression change as the name registered. Lisa crumpled up the paper and slammed both her palms down on the radar indicator board.

"I can't believe it! I just . . . I can't believe this! It's unbelievable!"

"What is it, Lisa?" Claudia was still playing dumb, and not very effectively.

"Don't be coy with me, Claudia. You've seen this list. How does Hunter rate a promotion to group leader?"

Claudia stroked her chin. "Uh, let's see, I think he was involved in some sort of rescue operation—"

"That's a matter of opinion, Claudia. Oh oh . . ."

Lisa was staring at the radar screen and fiddling with the control knobs. Claudia went over to her.

"What's up?"

She was working the dials, trying to tune something in. "I guess I shouldn't have slapped this thing so hard— it's all static."

"Try switching over to the backup overrides," Claudia suggested.

She did, but the static remained.

"I'm going to run this through computer analysis," said Lisa.

The two women waited for the system to display its diagnosis. They sucked in their breath when it appeared: It was a jamming pattern.

"Put us on yellow alert," Lisa said with newfound enthusiasm. "Notify all VT teams to report to their fighters and stand by."

Things at Minmei's party had gone from bad to worse, and for Rick, the yellow alert siren blaring in the streets of Macross City felt like a reprieve.

By the time he and his new cohorts had arrived at the party, the restaurant was already packed. In addition to scores of Veritech defenders and a few of Minmei's show business friends, the mayor and his cronies were circulating around, pressing the flesh. At times it seemed to Rick that Mayor Luan harbored some secret plan for Minmei, as if she was some pet project or secret weapon he was going to unleash on the world. Minmei, dressed to kill in her purple mandarin tunic was at her butterfly best flitting from table to table, center stage no matter where she was in the room. She was hard on Rick for arriving late. Moreover, he had forgotten to pick up a present. She was duly impressed with the new lieutenant's bars but an instant later had taken an immediate shine to shy Max and was at that very moment singing harmony with him to guitar accompaniment. And the mayor hadn't helped matters any when he came over to Rick and in a conspiratorial whisper warned him about letting Minmei get too far out of sight—"She seems quite taken with your new corporal, Rick"—as if Rick could influence what she did and where she went.

Rick had quickly become withdrawn and moody, noncommunicative even when Minmei's orbit took her past his table or her wink from across the room was meant to single him out as some sort of accomplice in her performance. Rick stayed close to the mildly intoxicating punch and kept his eyes down for most of the afternoon.

But then the alert had been sounded.

And now all the flyboys were gulping down their drinks and racing for the door, leaving Minmei standing alone, her song left unfinished, center stage stolen from her by the war. And even though Rick couldn't approve of her petulance and spoiled behavior, he couldn't help being moved by her innocence and naiveté. He wanted to run to her and promise her that this war would go away soon and that all her dreams would come true. But the best he could promise was his return later with the gift he had for her. He gave her his kerchief to wipe the tears from her face, and she put her arms around his neck and thanked him with a hug.

"What would I do without you, Rick?"

He pulled away from her embrace; Max and Ben were calling to him from the hexagonal doorway, motioning for him to get himself in gear—after all, there was a battle to be fought, a war to be waged!

"Come on, Lieutenant, we don't want to keep the enemy waiting, do we?"

Rick looked at Ben and felt a sudden urge to strangle him. *No*, he thought, *we mustn't keep them waiting*.

CHAPTER
EIGHT

One must now address the reasons for Khyron's failures. Was he defeated on each occasion by the Earth forces, or was he in fact defeated by his own commanders? So often recalled from the very brink of success; so often within reach of victory. Why wasn't he allowed full rein? Again, there is wide disagreement among the commentators we have been discussing throughout. Gordon (along with several of his psychohistorian disciples) wants to convince us that Dolza and Breetai had so misread Gloval's tactics as to believe that he would have destroyed the ship rather than allow it to fall into Zentraedi hands. And yet, Exedore himself has stated that: "...rivalry had completely splintered the Zentraedi high command. Continued contact with Human self-initiative had by this time fostered unrecognized and certainly incomprehensible competitive drives in the commanders themselves. Dolza, Breetai, and even Azonia (who had reasons of her own to behave otherwise) were unconsciously mimicking an emotion they had never experienced. 'For the greater glory of the Zentraedi' had already become an archaic phrase."

Rawlins, *Zentraedi Triumvirate: Dolza, Breetai, Khyron*

RICK, BEN, AND MAX—THE NEWLY FORMED Black Team—were ordered to defensive positions in the Fourth Quadrant, close to the fortress and too far from the main fighting to suit Dixon. He was anxious to get into the thick of it.

Below them, between the SDF-1 and Mars, Skull, Red, and the other squadrons were engaging enemy pods. From his vantage point, Rick could make out a cat's cradle of interlacing laser light punctuated by brief spherical flashes of death, but most of the battle information came to him via the aircom net. It was beginning to sound like the boys had the enemy on the run; indeed, the explosive bursts seemed to indicate that the pods had fallen back to positions closer to the planetary rim.

As the exchanges continued to diminish in size and frequency, Rick began to worry that Gloval was permitting the VTs to fly right into a trap, or worse, that he had ordered offensive action against one of the mother ships. Dixon was ready to join them nevertheless.

"Can't we get into some of that?" he wanted to know.

"We have our orders," Rick told him sharply. "Now, stick close to me and stay alert."

On the bridge of the SDF-1, Gloval was studying the deployment of pods and Veritechs on the threat board. The enemy was trying something new. Instead of assaulting the fortress, as was their usual routine, they were keeping their distance, perhaps fearful that the main gun had been repaired. *Would that that were the case*, thought Gloval. But the more he studied the screen, the more suspicious he grew. The enemy wasn't turning tail to avoid battle. Gloval shook his head in amusement. Did they really think him such a fool? It was obvious that they were hoping to lure the VTs away from the fortress in order to open up a second front.

He was ready to issue a recall order when new data verified his hunch.

Vanessa announced, "We have an attack force of enemy pods at our stern."

Gloval ordered that the Gladiator force be called up, and Dr. Lang was requested to shunt sufficient energy from the shields to arm the main batteries aft. The sec-

ond enemy wave was coming in from the relatively un-
guarded Fourth Quadrant, where Hunter's Black Team
was on defensive patrol. As this sector was put up on the
screen, the bridge crew readied themselves to render assistance.

Rick received the communiqué from the bridge and
moments later had the enemy assault team on his cockpit
radar display.

"Company's coming," he told Max and Ben. "Let's
show them how we treat party crashers."

Locked into the bridge command center, the three
Veritech pilots swung their fighters toward the advancing
pods. They were still too distant for visuals, but Rick
was soon facing those characteristic pinpoints of explosive light that signaled laser bombardment.

A nanosecond later the bolts reached them. Rick ordered his men to begin evasive maneuvers to lessen the
staying power of the charge. Some of his own circuits
were already fried, but it was nothing he needed to
worry about.

And then they had a visual on the pods: There were
only a dozen of them, including an Officer's Pod. They
came into the quadrant, weapons blazing, the Black
Team ready for them.

"I'm gonna fly rings around these guys, Lieutenant.
Just watch me go," Rick heard Ben say.

Dixon fired off a cluster of heat-seekers and attempted to roll out. But the enemy had outguessed him,
and two of the pods were following him through, positioning themselves on either side of his mecha well inside
the lethal cone.

"Break across that seven o'clock bandit, Ben," Rick
shouted into the net. "Don't get cute, they're going to
catch you in their cross fire!"

Dixon realized he was in trouble and called for an assist. The two pods were practically on top of him, pouring particle-beam energy at his booster pack. A Veritech could stand only a few seconds of this; ultimately, structural molecules would be altered and the ship would come apart. Ben would be fried alive.

Rick kicked in his aft boosters, found one of the pods in his reticle, and loosed two missiles. They caught the pod at its weakest spot, just where the cockpit cover was hinged to the main body of the sphere. The hatch blew open, precious atmosphere was released and the pilot inside clawed frantically at his controls. Soon the lifeless thing was drifting aimlessly out of the arena.

The second pod was still throwing heat into Dixon's fighter, but the pilot, realizing that *he* was now outnumbered, began to drop away.

"I'm going to save your skin, Ben. Just retro when I give the word." Rick haloed the ostrich and shouted, *"Now!"*

His thumb came down hard on the Hotas trigger. Two missiles dropped from their pylons and connected with the pod, blowing it to pieces.

While Ben was thanking him, Rick looked around for Max. There was a lot of activity going on off to his right; as Rick was soon to realize, Max was at the center of it.

The corporal had shifted to Battloid mode and was using the gatling cannon to take out pod after pod, executing evasive maneuvers the likes of which Rick had never seen. Max was pushing the Veritech into reverses Rick wouldn't have believed possible. He had heard about pilots who could totally surrender themselves to the alpha state, but he had never seen anything like this with his own eyes.

"Look at him go!" Dixon was yelling on the tac net.

Max had second sight, eyes behind his head, a sixth sense...the enemy mecha couldn't get near him. He was polishing off the last of the assault group, and Rick was on the horn congratulating him.

"I'm happy I was able to help out," came the humble reply. "Now I'll show you something I learned in flight school."

Rick was amazed: Max was literally about to *talk* Ben and him through a maneuver; it was difficult enough to control the complexities of the Veritech weapons system and answer to the demands of the mecha, but to have anything left over for movement, let alone human speech!...But here was Max, explaining every move as he went after two new entries. He drew the enemy in, then suddenly inverted himself, firing his thrusters so that he was coming right down their throats with his weapons blasting. The two pods were taken out, along with a third that had appeared at Rick's port side unannounced.

Rick's jaw went slack.

"It's called Fokker's Feint," said Max. "You have to confuse them. And while they're looking for you, you come up behind them and tap them on the back!"

Lisa Hayes was suddenly on the net at the same time, berating Rick for his poor response time. He offered as an excuse the two inexperienced pilots he had with him, listening to himself while watching Max execute a flourish of moves.

Maybe this was one of the advantages to being a superior officer, he thought. Foul up and you could lay the blame on your men; succeed, and their victories were your own.

* * *

Khyron was observing the progress of the battle from his Officer's Pod. The diversionary strategy wasn't working out exactly as he had hoped, but it had opened up a few holes in the fortress's defensive perimeter. Most of the Micronian mecha had been successfully lured far from Zor's ship, and those few remaining fighters were rapidly being eliminated. The second assault team had taken the sting out of the main batteries of the SDF-1, and the mecha dispatched to slow their attack had been eliminated. Now it was time for the coup de grace: Khyron's special elite assault team would storm the fortress and put an end to this game.

It was almost too easy...

Through his headset, Rick heard the voice of Lisa Hayes:

"Enemy forces have broken through our defenses in the Third Quadrant. You're our only hope, Black Leader."

"We're on our way," Rick told her.

Ben was out front, making up for lost time with continuous fire, little of it effective. Rick warned him not to waste his ammo. Max, meanwhile, took two pods off Rick's tail and asked Rick if it was all right to fire when it *wasn't* a waste. Rick ignored the joke and ordered Max and Ben to split up, hoping they could drive a wedge into the attacking enemy units.

Only a few of the Phalanx and close-in guns on the SDF-1 were capable of giving them cover fire, and most of those had sustained some damage. Destroids and Gladiators floated above the ship, pieces of debris, sparking out as they drifted toward oblivion.

Rick, already reaching out for the B mode lever, ordered his team to switch over to Battloid. He watched as the tailerons of Max's fighter folded down and the wings swept fully back to lock into place. Next, the entire undercarriage, including the twin aft thrusters, swung down and forward, riding on massive pins located beneath the cockpit module. As rear thruster sheaths chevroned to become the Battloid's feet, the ventral fuselage halves split away from each other and spread outward to form the arms. Hands slid out from armored compartments. Inside the mecha Max's seat would now be riding upward along a shaft that would reposition the pilot inside the head—a minute ago the undercarriage laser-gun bubble. Rick's own fighter was going through the same changes. He could sometimes feel his own body react, as though unseen hands were at work on him.

Thus reconfigured, the three members of the Black Team touched down on the SDF-1's hull and brought their gatlings to bear on incoming enemy pods. Ben stood his ground, screaming curses at the ostriches as they made their approach. Initially he was positioned near one of the damaged phalanx guns, his cannon at high port, but he stepped out into the open to trap-shoot an incoming bandit just as a second flew in from behind and dropped him with a blast that caught the Battloid full in the back. Rick winced and tried to raise him on the net.

"Ben, are you alive in there?"

Dixon answered weakly; he was hurt but had somehow managed to survive the hit.

Rick was moving in to lend a hand, when several pods appeared over the horizon of the ship. High-density transuranic slugs from the gatling brought two down. Two others loosed their rockets ineffectively and streaked overhead, but the Officer's Pod that led them seemed determined to go one on one with him. It was the second time that day that Rick was to witness incredible maneuvering.

The Officer's Pod—not spherical like the others but somewhat elongated and fishlike above its legs, with twin "hand-gun" arms and a top-mounted long-muzzled plastron cannon—toyed with him, dodging each of his shots as though the pilot inside could read Rick's mind. The pod leaped over a conning tower and came down behind him; Rick turned and fired, but the enemy was already spaceborne again and swooping in, clawed legs swinging back and forth, discharging rounds from its hand-guns.

Rick's mecha took several hits through the torso; then the glancing blow of a projectile sheared off the Battloid's left arm. Rick thought the damaged vehicle down to one knee as the enemy pod came in to finish him. When it was within reach, he brought the Battloid to its feet and used the useless cannon to bat at the thing. He connected, driving the ostrich into a spin that brought it crashing down to the surface of the ship, minus one of its own cannon appendages.

The two mecha faced each other across a distance of about 200 meters—a showdown on a western street. Rick worked frantically at the controls, trying to divert power from the main mechamorphosis systems into the main gun, but all his efforts proved futile. He stared out of the cockpit faceplate of the Battloid as the enemy manning the Officer's Pod raised the muzzle of the one good arm and prepared to fire...

Onboard the Zentraedi flagship Breetai was informed of the battle being waged against the SDF-1, in direct violation of his orders. He rushed from his quarters to the command bubble, where Exedore was waiting for him, watching images play across the projecbeam field with growing disgust.

"It is as I feared, Commander. Khyron has taken matters into his own hands once again."

Breetai stood, arms akimbo, regarding the action as explosive flashes of light reflected in his faceplate.

"So this is Khyron's idea of war games?" Breetai snorted. "Again he has the temerity to disobey my orders!"

"I suggest that we recall him . . . before he succeeds in destroying the ship."

"The fool, I warned him." Breetai turned away. "Use the nebulizer to override the astrogational systems of his attack force. We'll pull this offensive out from under him."

Exedore moved to the nebulizer controls. "Ready to initiate on your command."

"Mark!" Breetai shouted to the screen.

Warning lights were flashing on the bridge of the SDF-1. Sensors were picking up energy readings of an extraordinary type. Astrogational and engineering were reporting dangerous fluctuations in the drive systems; it was as if all control had been lost.

Meanwhile, on the skin of the ship, Khyron was taking aim at Rick's Battloid.

The Zentraedi commander felt the pod suddenly surrender itself to a higher power and knew at once what had happened: Breetai was recalling them. On the very brink of victory, and the fool was recalling them! He could do nothing; the nebulizer had even neutralized the weapon system of the pod. This fortunate Micronian pilot would live to fight another day, Khyron said to himself as the Officer's Pod rose involuntarily from the skin of Zor's ship. He could see the Battloid lift its head in some gesture of wonder or amazement and could only guess how the pilot inside was reacting

Rick would recall his feelings later, too stunned at the moment to analyze his reactions.

In the aftermission debriefing room they would all report the same thing: that the pods had suddenly abandoned their attack and lifted off, as though they had been given some sort of recall signal.

While Dr. Lang tried to postulate the cause of the strange readings he had received and Gloval asked himself why the enemy had called off its attack, Lieutenant Hunter had a private session with his two new charges in the mess hall of the *Prometheus*.

Ben's head was bandaged. On the positive side, it seemed that one of those blasts had finally gotten it through the corporal's thick skull that discretion was the better part of valor. Max, on the other hand, credited with at least nine kills, was basking in self-adulation, wondering only half in jest whether the brass might not end up promoting him from corporal to general overnight.

Still amazed by what he had seen Max accomplish during the battle, Rick found that his respect for his fellow pilot was marred by feelings of jealousy. But he was too exhausted to dwell on it; he had just enough residual energy to carry him to his quarters. He was already thinking about crawling into his bunk and courting sleep.

An hour later he was standing in the doorway to his room, reaching in to hit the light switch. One step inside and his eyes fixed on the bed and the invitation laying there, paste-on red heart seal still unbroken. He groaned: Minmei's birthday present! It was like a bad dream, like being up in your Veritech and suddenly realizing you'd forgotten to ammo up.

Rick started pacing the room, trying to recall the mental list of gift possibilities he'd composed earlier. What was it—shoes, jewelry, clothes? He checked his watch: twenty-two thirty. He knew he didn't stand a chance, but he had to give it a go.

He rode an empty tube into Macross City and ran up and down the streets searching for an open store, cursing EVE with every step, because before these artificial sunrises and sunsets the city had rocked twenty-four hours a day. Now you were lucky if you stumbled on a place that served hamburgers past midnight. Then he spied a robo-vending machine on one corner and called to it; he would swear that the thing turned and looked at him before streaking away. Why did they do this? Rick asked himself as he gave chase. Human and animated robo-vendor ran for several blocks through the late-night deserted streets of Macross, Rick calling out to it, pleading with it, and ultimately cursing it. But the device managed to outrun him.

He caught his breath and began heading in the general direction of Minmei's apartment above the White Dragon. He was going to have to tell her something— *anything* but the truth: that he'd been too busy doing battle with the enemy to get her a gift. Of course, there was a chance that she was already asleep. Maybe he would just sort of lurk around underneath the balcony of her apartment, see if there were any lights on up there . . .

As if on cue, though, she came to the window, saw

him out there under the streetlight, and threw open the balcony doors, calling to him.

"Rick, I knew you wouldn't forget." She was checking her wristwatch. "Five minutes to go. What did you bring me?"

He started to trip over his words. "Well, look, Minmei, about your present, you see, I was planning . . . er, that is, what I meant to tell you before . . ."

She laughed. "Come on, Rick, don't be a jerk. I don't care what you brought me. It's the thought that counts. Now, throw it up here. Come on."

Rick's arms fell to his sides in a gesture of complete helplessness. But his right hand had found the boxed Medal of Valor in his trousers pocket. He pulled it out and regarded it in the streetlight. The brass had given him this to single him out; it said: Listen, you are something special, you've been of extraordinary service to all of us in this war we're waging, wear this and be proud, wear this and be recognized by your fellow comrades.

So why couldn't it say the same thing to her: By giving it to her he was saying that *she* was really the special one, that his bravery and valor were in her honor, that she was his inspiration, the person he returned to—*the reason he returned*.

He snapped the lid closed and gave the box an underhand toss toward her outstretched hands. He couldn't see her face well enough to judge her reaction, and for a moment the silence unnerved him. But when she spoke, he was certain there was no insincerity in her voice.

"Rick, I don't know if I can accept this. Really . . ."

"I want you to have it, Minmei. It—it says what I can't say to you. Please, keep it."

She held the box to her cheek. "It's beautiful, and I love it."

Rick smiled. "Happy birthday."

She blew him a kiss and waved good night.

Rick waited until the lights went out, then walked the quiet streets of Macross City. It was peaceful and pleasant. Dogs barked in the distance and laughter filtered out of open doorways. It was almost like real life.

CHAPTER
NINE

There are so many wonderful things going on in my life, it's sometimes hard to believe it can continue like this. But what would the people of Macross City think of me if I announced to them that getting stuck in the fold and landing out here in deep space was one of the greatest things that ever happened to me? Aunt Lena and Uncle Max's restaurant is really happening; even the mayor comes to eat there. I have three complete songs written: "My Boyfriend's a Pilot," "Stagefright," and "To Love." My dance instructor and my voice coach tell me that I'm making excellent progress, and I'm actually even thinking of sending in an application for the Miss Macross pageant. But I know that I could never be accepted! That is just too wild a dream to come true—even for me!... The only rough spot in my life right now is Rick, and I can't figure out what to do about him. I owe him my life, for real; but he wants me to be something I can never be: a loyal girlfriend, maybe someone who would be content to live in his shadow. But I have shadows of my own to cast!

From the diary of Lynn-Minmei

As THE MAYOR OF MACROSS CITY, TOMMY LUAN had a lot to deal with. For a long time after the spacefold he harbored a fear that the population was one day going to wake from the collective shock of the experience and he'd have a mass riot on his hands. But that never came about. It was probably an indication of how inured the human race had become to tragedy; ten years of global war had started it, and the arrival of the SDF-1 from deep space, carrying with it evidence of extraterrestrial life forms, had sealed it. But in any case the residents of Macross City were a breed apart from the start.

Tommy Luan had been part of the second wave of newcomers to arrive on Macross Island. The first consisted mainly of scientific and military representatives from the newly formed World Unification Alliance, Dr. Lang and his group, Gloval, Fokker, Colonel Edwards, and others from the supercarrier *Kenosha*. Then there followed the decision to attempt a construction of the ship—"the Visitor," as it was called—and this brought in the numerous tech teams who were really Macross City's founding fathers. Luan was one of these. His background was construction—immense projects: bridges, skyscrapers, hospitals—no job was too large. But the Global Civil War had put an end to an unprecedented period of growth in the building trades, and like far too many others Luan was on the skids and looking for a job. He applied for a position on the Macross project and was accepted. He received a security clearance and once on the island found himself placed in charge of housing construction for the tech and support groups.

As the SDF-1 began to take shape, so did Macross City. The ongoing project to decipher and apply the principles of Robotechnology became the one to try for; Macross Island became a haven for scientists from every discipline, pacifists and idealists disheartened by continued war fare, Senator Russo's military teams, and the support network that grew up to house, feed, and entertain these various groups.

Tommy Luan built Macross City, no one would have taken issue with that; so when it came time to call Macross City what it was and elect officials, Tommy Luan won hands down. And four years later, when the city had grown to a population of over 100,000, Tommy Luan would still be on top.

And now, months after the fold, here was Tommy Luan still in charge. The fact that the city and most of its inhabitants had been rescued was miraculous; what had been done to the city since was equally so. For a time it had been like living in a giant's cellar; enormous conduits and pipes overhead, bulkheads for horizons, the eerie sounds of the ship permeating the city. There was room enough for the 50,000 survivors, but a kind of collective claustrophobia prevailed.

Then there was the disaster that befell them during the first modular transformation and the continued attacks on the SDF-1 by their unseen enemy. But Macross City had weathered it all, and the new city was a marvel to behold. Constructed on three levels that ascended to the massive starport dome, the city had everything it had had on Earth—and then some. There were streets (even hills), shopping malls, electric cars and trucks, a monorail, tube and lift systems, several movie theaters, arcades, an amphitheater, even a radio station. The engineers who had come up with Eve—Enhanced Video Emulation—were experimenting with the blue skies, sunrises, and sunsets. And soon the Macross Broadcasting System would be inaugurated.

But there was an important something missing: There was no news.

Except, of course, what they were *permitted* to broadcast to the population concerning the war. Births and deaths; no crime to speak of; no traffic accidents; no corruption. There was no real life sense to the place; some fear and paranoia, but no real fun or excitement.

Which is precisely why Mayor Tommy Luan had jumped at the idea of running a Miss Macross pageant when Jan Morris's people had approached him.

Jan Morris's people——her agent, her manager, her publicity agent, the whole lot of them along with the noted Hollywood star—had become overnight residents of Macross City since the spacefold. She had been part of a variety show organized in the States and newly arrived on Macross Island to take part in the Launching Day celebration. Now Macross City had the whole show on a permanent basis; in addition to Jan Morris, there was an entire show band, two rock groups, two stand-up comics, and three singers. The Morris group presented the idea of the beauty pageant with real humanitarian zeal: Macross City needed a little excitement, and what better way to inaugurate the new television station than with a knock-'em-dead show with plenty of beautiful women and production numbers. Macross Island had been gearing up for just such an event, but what Morris's people were proposing was not a beauty pageant in the traditional sense of the term—Jan's people knew better than to put their star up against seventeen-year-olds in a swimsuit competition—but more of a Miss Popularity contest based on each individual's contributions to the spirit and growth of the transplanted city. The way they had it figured, Jan would be crowned with the title at the end of the show and everyone would walk away happy.

The mayor had listened patiently to their plan, all the while formulating some thoughts of his own. It was a terrific idea—Macross City could use the boost, any excuse to gather behind an issue that wasn't war-related—but he saw through their motives: It was true that Jan, like so many others, had done her share to keep up the morale in the city, but as an actress (and only a fair one at that) in a world without movies, what else *could* she do but play on her past? But now with the SDF-1 through the launch window and the actual final leg of the ship's homeward journey a real possibility, it was time to think about the future of Jan Morris as a marketable property. After all, her audiences on Earth had surely regretted her loss, and just as surely they had moved on by now. So unless Jan Morris could return to Earth singled out by a title like Miss Macross from the other 50,000 returnees, her future as a star would be bleak. She would have missed her personal launch window.

With the right publicity, Jan Morris would certainly be a shoe-in for the title. But Mayor Tommy Luan didn't want to see that happen. Jan Morris was deserving enough, but her image was all wrong; she represented the past, and moreover, she was not really a *voluntary* resident of the city. No, what Macross City needed was someone whom they could call their own; not just a figurehead but some young woman who would embody the spirit of adventure and survival, of victory and hope.

The Morris group continued to lay out their plans, but unknown to them, the mayor had already chosen the winner. *She would be perfect!* he told himself. Not only was she of mixed background and ancestry, lovely to look at, personable, and talented, but she was already a minor celebrity in her own right. For two weeks she and her young lieutenant friend had faced an ordeal in the bowels of the ship; it was her family that had reopened the first restaurant in the resurrected city, the White Dragon; and the flyboys all adored her. Yes, she would be perfect, the mayor decided:

Lynn-Minmei, Miss Macross!

* * *

Rick was having lunch with Minmei at Variations, a popular eatery on the upper tier of Macross City, when she told him about her entry in the Miss Macross pageant. They had been seeing each other frequently during the past two months. The enemy had pulled back for some reason, and the ship was on a course that would return them to Earth in six months or so. In general, things had been going well, but this was the first definite news Rick heard of the resuscitated contest, and he was speechless; it was hard enough sharing her with half the Robotech Defense Force, and now she was on the brink of becoming the communal property of the entire SDF-1!

"Rick, please don't get like that," she responded to his silence. "The mayor went ahead and entered me without even asking. And besides, you know how much this means to me."

"What are you, his secret weapon or something? I mean, what about *us*, Minmei? I mean . . . oh, forget it, I don't know what I mean."

She reached across the table for his hand. "Listen, Rick, will you be there for me—you and Roy and the guys? I'm going to need all the help I can get."

He looked into her blue eyes and began to feel the anger leaving him. His smile brought one to her face.

"Of course we'll be there. We're on standby patrol that night, but Roy will able to pull some strings. Anyway, you're going to win that contest hands down."

"You really think I have a chance?"

"You're a sure thing," he told her. "You *are* our secret weapon, don't you know that?"

After Rick left the restaurant, Minmei ordered more tea for herself and stared out at Macross City's experimental blue skies. *A sure thing*, she mused. If only that were true, if only she could have the confidence that others had in her. The mayor, for one; he was treating her like she'd already *won* the contest, building up her chances, seeing to it that she had enough money for a new outfit. But what chance did she stand against girls like Hilary Rockwell and Shawn Blackstone? Let alone Jan Morris! Hey, Jan Morris was her *idol*!

Minmei's hands fell to her lap. She looked down at her plaid school skirt, the blazer and tie. She thought she saw herself as she really was: just a kid with big dreams. A kid who needed constant attention and encouragement, even when she hated herself for bringing that about. At war with herself: one half weak and scared and full of self-doubts, against a constantly charming, vivacious, confident other half. The former could not for an instant sustain the dream that she would win, while the latter self seemed to embrace that dream as if it was something *meant to be*—destined.

Well, wasn't it enough, she asked herself, just to be a part of the pageant, among those others she looked up to?

The answer was a resounding *no*!

The Macross amphitheater (the Star Bowl, as it was affectionately known) was located at the extreme edge of the enormous hold that housed the city. When planning the amphitheater, Robotech architects and engineers had taken full advantage of a preexisting bowl-shaped depression in the ship's floor and a lage spacelight in the ceiling above the building site. The result was about as close to an open-air theater as one could hope for aboard a spaceship. The Star Bowl could seat 30,000, and there wasn't an empty place to be found on the night of the pageant.

The Macross Broadcasting System had labored long and hard to position their cameras for maximum coverage of the event. If all went as planned, the other 20,000 residents would be able to view the pageant from their shops, homes, or any of the curbside monitors that had recently been installed throughout the city.

The host for the show was Ron Trance, a veteran of countless benefit and rear-line shows for the troops during the Global Civil War. Trance had been slated to run the SDF-1 launch celebration and had been caught up in the fold. The seven judges included Colonel Maistroff and Captain Gloval, the editor of the newspaper, a former advertising executive, and three officials from the mayor's office; but these seven were a mere formality—they would handle the contestants' questions and choose the semifinalists but would cast no final votes. That voting would be left to the people of Macross City. Each seat in the arena had been equipped with a sensor that would transmit a vote during balloting, and those in the city could cast their votes by phone or at any of several dozen voting booths.

Minmei's cheering section was seated to the left of the central runway, along the midsection of the amphitheater. Roy and his Skull Team were there, along with the members of Rick's newly formed Vermilion. Other squads were scattered throughout the area. The young lieutenant himself had yet to arrive.

The mayor opened the show, and after a few technical glitches the pageant got under way. The orchestra performed a piece written especially for the pageant, lasers crisscrossed overhead through colored smoke, spotlights played across the stage, and a series of holoprojected letters assembled themselves above to spell out "Miss Macross!" To thunderous applause Ron Trance made his entry, hoofing and singing. The curtains parted, and the twenty-eight contestants strutted on stage in a simple choreographed parade. The grand prizes were announced: a recording contract, a screen test, and a new fanliner, "the latest thing in sports mecha...featuring the powerful new VA hydro-turbine engine, designed by Ikkii Takemi himself..."

Minmei was comfortable with this part of the show. She hadn't realized that the bright lights at the front of the stage would make it impossible for her to see the audience, but it was probably just as well: It was more dreamlike this way, and she felt that she possessed more control over fantasy than real life. But backstage later on, the frights began to take hold of her. All week long she had been coached by her chaperons and support group on how to act during the next portions of the event, but just now she couldn't recall one bit of their advice. So she relied instead on Uncle Max's words: "Just be yourself."

It was while everyone was running around making costume changes for the upcoming poise and question portions of the show that she spotted Jan Morris.

Minmei had been trying to meet her all week long, but Jan's agents had kept her inaccessible. She was the real star of the show, Minmei supposed, and here she was, just one of the contestants, a few seats away talking to her manager. She certainly was pretty, though—blond curls piled by a black and white striped headband, long legs, gorgeous blue dress with red horizontal bands, and that million-dollar smile. But as Minmei overcame her shyness and drew nearer, pen and memo book in hand, to ask for an autograph, she couldn't help but notice that

Jan was a lot older than most of the girls and a lot shorter than she appeared to be in her films.

She was also upset about something.

Jan's manager was saying, "I guess they put you at the head of the list because you're the only star. But I've talked them into calling you last."

"Oh, thanks a bunch, Mary." Jan's voice dripped sarcasm.

"Listen, Jan, it's only right that you—"

"Will you stop it, please!" the actress snapped. "This isn't Hollywood. I didn't ask to go to the ... planets! Or get stuck in this oversized sardine can."

"So why are we doing this? We don't have to participate in this thing, Jan."

Jan just stared at her. "It goes with the territory, sweetheart. You should know that. I mean, someday we're going to get back home, and I'm not about to play the forgotten star—"

She glanced up at that moment and saw Minmei standing there.

"Now what?" Jan muttered.

"Excuse me, Miss Morris, I'm really one of your biggest fans, and so I was wondering if you'd be kind enough to give me your autograph." Minmei pushed the memo book forward. "I'm afraid this is all I have to write on, though. Would it be all right?"

Jan Morris gave her a cold once-over and, suddenly on the verge of tears, declined. Mary interceded before Minmei could apologize. "If you want an autograph from a *real* star, get yourself a real autograph book." Jan Morris stood up, and the two of them walked away.

Minmei was stunned by the encounter, but she didn't have a moment to think about it: Center stage was calling.

Rick arrived at the amphitheater just in time to catch Minmei's grand entrance. Macross City's mass transit system was so jammed, he'd had to bicycle over from his quarters. He took a seat in the balcony, his binoculars zeroed in on the runway.

Minmei wore a hand-woven lavender mandarin gown of clinging silk, a dress that had belonged to her grandmother and had been altered to suit the girl's slim figure and long legs. The tunic had a simple round collar, flawless embroidery over the left shoulder, and revealing slits. She wore matching pumps and had strands of pink cultured pearls in her braided and bunned hair. Rick thought she looked fantastic as she stepped forward into the bright spot to wait for the judges' questions.

"Could we have your thoughts about the war and the needs of Macross City, your hopes for the future, your ambitions . . ."

Rick was simply too taken with the sight of her to pay much attention to Minmei's responses, but just then Captain Gloval asked a relevant question: "Do you have a steady boyfriend among all the fighter pilots you count as your friends?"

Rick hung on her every word.

"I don't believe I'm ready for that at this point. I mean, I think it's best to have a lot of different friends."

Colonel Maistroff followed up: "Do you find it difficult having male friends?"

Minmei laughed. "Not at all! In fact, I have one really good friend who's just like a brother to me."

Rick slapped himself in the forehead with the heel of his hand. *A brother?! A BROTHER?!!* And just then, while Minmei was taking in the applause, his pager went off. He raised his eyes to the starlight, wondering who was calling him out this time.

CHAPTER
TEN

"Rome wasn't built in a day—Macross City was!"

Mayor Tommy Luan

Had it not been for the Miss Macross pageant, I might never have undertaken the journey which led me to enlightenment—a journey I hope to guide you through in the pages that follow. It was only after I had opened my heart to the First Truth—that beauty and fame were not only transitory but illusory—that my soul was sufficiently prepared to accept the profound wisdom of the heavens: the knowledge that we are but seeds in the cosmic garden, potential given form and the will to evolve, true children of the stars— beings of noble light!

Jan Morris, *Solar Seeds, Galactic Guardians*

WHEN ACCOUNTS OF THE FIRST ROBOTECH WAR were finally written, not one of that war's many chroniclers failed to point out the curious turn of events precipitated by the Miss Macross pageant. The word "irony" appears often in those accounts, but irony is a judgment rendered after the fact and, in the case of Lynn-Minmei and the part she would come to play in the hostilities, much too simple and soft a term.

Exedore could no longer allow his growing concerns about the Micronians to go unspoken. The Tritani pattern was being woven again, and although it was not the

Zentraedi way to look back, the application of lessons from the past was now essential. Otherwise the quadrant would surely fall to the vengeful *Invid*!

Just when events had calmed somewhat—Khyron was temporarily reined in and Dolza had issued an order allowing the SDF-1 a brief stay of execution—the Earthlings had once again demonstrated their penchant for the unpredictable.

Strange, incomprehensible telecommunications were being broadcast from the dimensional fortress. Exedore had requested that Commander Breetai meet with him on the bridge.

The audio and visual signals were being broadcast on a relatively low-frequency wavelength; reception was intermittent at best. But even strong and continuous, they would have remained equally baffling to the Zentraedi commander and his adviser. What they saw were images of female Micronians undergoing what appeared to be an unusual metamorphosis, complete with bizarre changes in chroma and an alarming lack of any cause-and-effect sequencing. Breetai and Exedore stared at the screen and turned to each other with confused looks.

"'Miss . . . Macross . . . pageant' . . . What does it mean, Exedore?"

"I understand the individual words, Commander, but the meaning of it escapes me."

"A call for reinforcements, perhaps."

"No, Commander. The signal is far too weak for that."

Breetai experienced a moment of disquiet. Had he overlooked something important in the legends—something about a secret weapon the Micronians possessed, an innate ability to conquer all who threatened them?

"We must decipher this code, whatever it is. Have

you been successful in your efforts to teach our agents the Micronian tongue?"

"As successful as can be expected, Commander. They aren't—"

"Ready one of the Cyclops recon ships. Tell your operatives to stand by."

"M'lord," said Exedore, and backed away.

While his adviser was left to carry out the orders, Breetai studied the screen; there was something disturbing about those partially clothed and strangely colored females, a power about them that pierced him like an ancient arrow.

As regimented as the Zentraedi were, there were still individual personality types, and the three agents chosen to man the Cyclops recon were to prove as pivotal in the unfolding of events as the Miss Macross pageant itself. At the helm of the arachnidlike vessel was Rico, a wiry, effectively one-eyed warrior with a thin, sunken face, prominent cheekbones, and chiseled features. Bron, a beefy, powerful man with greasy red hair, was the navigator, and in charge of communications was Konda, a nondescript second lieutenant with shaggy, lavender hair well suited to current Earth fashions.

They'd been given a dangerous assignment: The Cyclops had to be brought in close enough to Zor's ship to monitor and record the curious Micronian broadcasts while at the same time evading detection. But Rico was an experienced surveillance pilot, and he soon had the Cyclops well situated for reception. He was not, however, prepared for what greeted his eyes (nor would he be for quite some time to come): Here was a Micronian male wearing some sort of strange devices in front of his eyes, holding in his hand an equally unusual device which he seemed to be directing toward . . . a *female*! An unclothed female at that! A-and the two of them were actually *together*—in the same space!

"This is unthinkable!" he cried.

Bron and Konda were similarly appalled.

Rico adjusted the recording controls to enhance the monitor image. "She must be wearing some new type of armor."

Bron disagreed: The armor covered the female's hips and breasts only; it didn't make sense.

"Perhaps those are the only vulnerable parts of a Micronian female," Rico offered.

"It's not armor at all," said Konda. "It's a formal uniform."

Bron shook his head. "You're both wrong. It's not even a female. It must be a secret weapon designed to *look* like one!"

Rick Hunter was missing the swimsuit competition.

He cursed his luck and muttered to himself while he strapped into the cockpit module of the armored Battloid. Why did Henricks have to pick tonight to get sick, and why did Rick's name have to appear at the top of the patrol list?

He had already gotten into an argument with Commander Hayes—"As primary patrol backup, you should have remained on the base, Lieutenant Hunter, not run off to some foolish beauty pageant!"—and now Minmei was going to be disappointed that he'd missed her big moment. "This sucks!" he yelled to the techs who were operating the module cranes and servos. They had one eye fixed on getting Rick's module into position and the other glued to monitors tuned in to the Miss Macross broadcast. No doubt Lisa Hayes and the SDF-1 bridge crew were doing the same. Meanwhile, Rick Hunter gets to go out into space and search for some enemy ship picked up on the long-range scanners.

Alone!

But if that was the way it had to be, he was going to recon in style, and the armored Battloid was just the ticket.

Still classified as experimental, it was the latest innovation from the Robotech Weapons Division. In addition to the standard armaments and defensive systems of the phase one design, the Battloid was equipped with new generation boosters and retros—the so-called deep-space augmentation pack—multiple-warhead "pectoral" launchers, and ejectable Bohrium-plated armor on those areas previously considered to be "vulnerable to penetration" by the boys in the RWD.

Rick spent a few moments familiarizing himself with the new controls. Fewer foot pedals, that was a plus. A new Hotas design—the hands on throttle and stick—improved ADF and ADI, totally useless before in deep space; a horizontal situation indicator—*ha!*; and a triple-screened TED, stocked with an up-to-date library of alien craft signatures. Rick donned the "thinking cap" and thought the mecha through some simple maneuvers. He then walked it cautiously to the *Prometheus* bay and launched himself from the fortress.

This was deep-space patrol once again, Mars just a memory. But there was some security to be gained from the sight of Sol, blazing bright in the heavens. It was almost beginning to feel like home turf out here.

Rick engaged the power pack boosters and relaxed back into the padded seat, locking onto the coordinates furnished him by the bridge. The enemy ship was thought to be a recon ship patrolling the outer limits of the SDF-1's sensor range.

The comtone sounded through his headset, and the face of Lisa Hayes appeared on the left commo screen. By the look of her, she was disturbed about something. In fact, she was livid.

"Lieutenant Hunter, who issued you permission to take out the armored Battloid? You are supposed to be flying ghost support, not confrontational."

Rick winced as the commander's words rushed out. "Excuse me, sir, but I'm out here on my lonesome, up against some—"

"We'll discuss this later, Lieutenant! Prepare to receive new coordinates."

Rick switched the ADF from lock to standby, but the data transfer was incomplete. The displays shut down, and the monitor was suddenly nothing but static lines and snow. Even audio was getting shaky. Rick heard something about "Zenny's fast food." He flipped the toggle to automatic fine-tuning.

"Some sort . . .-ust interference," Lisa was saying. "I'm . . .-witch . . . laser induction. Stand by."

Lisa's face faded and disappeared, replaced by the curvaceous form of Sally Forester walking the Star Bowl runway in a yellow two-piece.

Well, well, thought Rick, relaxing again, *the latest in diversion technique for the battle-weary fighter pilot*. Then Lisa was back on-line for an instant, instructing him to switch over to channel D-3. He tried that, but video reception seemed to be locked on the MBS transmissions. *Tough luck*, Rick said to himself, rubbing his hands together and grinning. It was Hilary Rockwell now, looking choice in her blue suit. Rough decision ahead; *almost easier to be up here*, Rick thought.

And then Minmei was on stage.

It was certainly one of the oddest feelings Rick had experienced in a while: Here he was in deep space, and there was Minmei in her teal bathing suit. As his spirits began to improve, the mecha responded; the Battloid was practically doing pirouettes in space! But the mood was to be short-lived: The console displays were flashing wildly, not out of contagious joy but because heat-seeking missiles had locked onto his tail!

Quickly, Rick commenced evasive action and instructed the stealth systems to launch ghosts. The rear cameras gave him a glimpse of his deadly pursuers—a flock of A/As—and sure enough, the scanners had picked up, registered, and catalogued the enemy vessel. A schematic formed on the port commo screen, profiles, front and rear views, weapons systems, vulnerable spots, suggested response. RECON VESSEL: CYCLOPS TYPE.

Rick fired the boosters and put the Battloid through its paces, pushing it for all it was worth while the heat-seekers continued to narrow the gap. So much for the ghosts. Concerned about their own survival, the warning systems were shouting out instructions, breaking his concentration. He shut down the interior audio supply and looked inside himself for the tone. A cold sweat broke out all over him. He thought the mecha left, right, up, down, and every which way but loose. The missiles were still with him.

And all the while, Minmei was parading across his three screens. They were flashing her measurements, for Pete's sake!

Rick was leading the missiles on a merry chase, but one that was going to have a most unfortunate ending unless he pulled something out of the hat—fast! Fratricide was his only hope. Desperately, he willed the Battloid to turn itself face to face with the heat-seekers and raised the gatling cannon; locking the targeting coordinator onto the leader of the pack, he fired!

Minmei stood in the wings, trembling. But when her name and contestant number were announced, all the anxiety seemed to leave her; she threw her shoulders back, stood straight and tall, and strutted on stage. She knew she looked good—the teal-colored stretch suit fit her perfectly—and given the audience reaction to her previous appearances, she figured she at least had a shot at one of the runner-up positions. If she could only keep it together for the next few minutes . . .

Her legs were shaking. She felt very unsteady on the high heels; she understood the need for them—added height and their pleasing effect on body posture—but she was unaccustomed to them. Nevertheless, she made it down to the end of the runway without incident. She had made her turn and was starting back, when it happened.

In thinking about it later, she would recall that the heel of her left shoe didn't so much let go as completely disappear as if it had been blown out from under her. But at the moment all she could think about was the embarrassment and the agony of defeat. Two pageant officials came to her aid and helped her up. There was some laughter from the audience, but mostly concern. And she did her best to alleviate that by demonstrating she was a trooper: She put on her best smile and hobbled her way back to center stage. The applause didn't end until long after she reached the wings.

Shawn Blackstone, who had become her close friend during the pageant, was at her side in a flash. She made light of the incident and said that it would have no effect on the judging.

"It shows them you're human, Minmei. Not like you-know-who."

You-know-who was Jan Morris, now making her walk down the runway to cheers and applause as Minmei watched from the wings. Jan was completely self-possessed; she'd been there a hundred times already. She wore a bold, striped suit with a halter top, more daring and revealing than the suits worn by the rest of the contestants—revealing enough to show some stretch marks, Minmei noticed.

Jan stood at the end of the runway taking it in; she had them eating out of her hand. Minmei couldn't watch. She turned aside, the contest over.

Time to wake up.

"You haven't beaten me yet, chumps!" Rick shouted to the stars.

The detonation of the heat-seekers had shaken him up and fried some of the Battloid's circuitry, but he was intact. Fortunately (and puzzlingly), the enemy had not followed up their initial attack. And now it was Rick's turn. He had a fix on the ship and launched enough missiles to wipe out a fleet.

Inside the Cyclops recon ship, the three Zentraedi operatives were so transfixed by the swimsuit competition that they almost failed to react to the counterattack. On the monitors were all those Micronian females, scantily clad (in armor or uniform, depending on whom you listened to), parading themselves in front of an enormous audience. It just had to be a weapons demonstration; why else would so many people gather in one place?

And one of the females had fallen. Uncertain if this

was part of the ceremony or not, the three began to focus on the fallen one to the exclusion of all else. Something was stirring in each of them—a novel feeling, confused as though half remembered from a previous life, disturbing but strangely appealing.

In fact, it took Rick's missiles to bring them to their senses. The Cyclops took the full force of the explosions and sustained heavy damage, but the weapons system had not been affected. Rico ordered visuals on the source of the missiles and returned fire. He watched the Micronian pilot throw the Battloid into a series of successful evasive maneuvers. Then, without warning, the pilot blew the armor from the ship and swung the Battloid toward them, gatling cannon blasting away.

Rico recognized a no-win situation when he saw one; sacrificing the ship for the crew was not something normally allowed by the Zentraedi command, but this was an important mission, and Rico thought it prudent to do so. With the Battloid still on the approach, he initiated the self-destruct sequence, then ordered his men to the escape pod.

Inside the Battloid cockpit, Rick engaged the foot thrusters and willed the mecha's legs forward; he was hurtling toward the enemy ship now, bent at the waist, feet stretched out in front of him.

Upon contact with the recon ship, he grappled on and used the feet to batter his way through the forward bays and into the ship's control station. He was actually seated on the instrument console when he brought up the cannon once again, but by then the crew had already abandoned ship. He raised the Battloid and walked it forward cautiously. A hatchway slammed shut somewhere, and all at once, off to his right, a bank of porthole monitors lit up, Minmei's face on each of the dozen screens.

She was the last image in Rick's mind when the ship exploded.

From the twenty-eight contestants the judges chose five finalists; Minmei was among them. They were seated in the center of the stage now, Shawn and Hilary on Minmei's right, Sally and Jan Morris on her left. Vertical light bars computer-linked to the voting processor rose behind each of them. Ron Trance was speaking. The big moment had arrived.

"And now, ladies and gentleman . . ." Ron milked it a bit, playing on the suspense, walking to and fro, cordless mike in hand. "It is time for *you* to decide who will be crowned *Miss Macross*! So get ready to cast your vote."

There was a moment of undiluted silence before Trance gave the word. Then the orchestra began a soft and slow build that quieted the murmurings from the audience and kept time with the ascending columns of light. Minmei wanted desperately to turn around, but she felt glued to her chair. The orchestra continued to pour out an atonal modulation which strained for a crescendo, the audience began to cheer and scream, the light rose higher and higher . . .

Some of those who were fortunate enough to have been there recall that Jan Morris was rising from her chair when Ron Trance made the final announcement. But it was Lynn-Minmei's chair that he approached, her hand that he took, her song he sang.

Minmei's recollection of the events was poorer than most; try as she might when viewing the tapes afterward, she could not recall her thoughts. All she remembered was the cape that had been draped over her shoulders, the crown placed upon her head, and the fact that when she looked up toward the starlight, it had seemed to her that unseen eyes were upon her, as though the stars themselves had ceased their motion to pay tribute to her moment.

Rick was semiconscious in the cockpit of the drifting disabled Battloid. The damaged instrument panels were flashing out, filling the small space with stroboscopic light. Shafts of pain radiated through him as he fought to reach the surface. Once there, a beatific creature appeared to him, and he felt a glimmer of hope. It wore a beautiful smile, a crown, and resplendent robe of many colors; it carried a scepter and stood proud and tall . . .

Rick Hunter, however, had strong survival instincts. He managed to reach forward through his stupor and activate the mecha's distress and self-guidance systems. Performing that act brought him around to full consciousness, and at once he realized the the Battloid was still receiving transmissions from the SDF-1. The angel who had visited his vision was none other than Minmei.

Lynn-Minmei, now Queen of Macross.

Rick watched as she surrendered herself to the audience. He reached toward the monitor as though he might touch her one last time before she passed beyond him forever, a part of something that would always be bigger than both of them.

Rick let his head loll forward.

What good was it to wake up to a world he could never enter?

"You have to look at things from our perspective: An alien armada appears in lunar orbit and launches an attack on Macross Island, the site of the SDF-1 reconstruction project; Captain Gloval, the fortress, and the entire island disappear. The aliens give chase to the ship and leave us alone. Then a year goes by and Gloval makes contact, informing us all of a sudden that he's returning the fortress to Earth, along with 50,000 people who were supposed to have perished during a volcanic eruption. What else were we supposed to tell the planet—that giant aliens had attacked and might or might not be back? And in addition to this, Gloval still had the armada on his tail, and he's leading the enemy back to Earth! I put it to you, who in their right mind would grant him permission to land? You might just as well invite catastrophe . . ."

Admiral Hayes, as quoted in Lapstein's *Interviews*

RICO, BRON, AND KONDA WERE BROUGHT BEFORE Breetai and Exedore for debriefing. They had escaped death at the hands of the Micronian ace but had failed to return to the Zentraedi mother ship with any substantial information regarding the unusual transmissions from the SDF-1. As a consequence, their lives were once again in jeopardy.

Breetai regarded the three operatives from his lofty position above the floor of the interrogation chamber. The debriefing was going nowhere fast, and he was tempted to put an end to it, but he decided to give it one last chance.

"We will review this again. What did you see?"

Once more the three commenced their explanations simultaneously.

"They were wearing military costumes—"

"It was armor—"

"Just looking at them gave me the strangest feeling—"

"Silence!" yelled Breetai. "It's apparent that none of you know what you saw."

In response to their salute, Breetai folded his arms across his chest and turned to his adviser. Exedore concurred with his plan to send out a second recon unit but went further in suggesting that it might be advantageous at this point to capture one or two of the Micronians alive.

"To what end?" Breetai wanted to know.

"To examine them, my lord. To determine for ourselves if they possess any knowledge of *Protoculture*."

Exedore whispered the word.

Breetai considered it. He was directing his thoughts toward Commander-in-Chief Dolza's possible reactions, when another argument broke out below him. Each of the pilots was certain of what he had seen. It was most curious: armor, military costume, a secret weapon disguised as a partially clad Micronian female . . .

Breetai allowed the bickering to escalate somewhat, but put a stop to it when physical blows were exchanged. Then he brought his massive fist down on the curved railing of the balcony.

"Enough of this! You were given an assignment, and you bungled it." He made a dismissive gesture. "Return to your quarters and await my judgment."

The pilots bowed and exited, leaving Breetai and his adviser alone in the chamber. Exedore had adopted a pensive pose.

"Of late I have witnessed this same scene all too frequently, Commander. Continued contact with these Micronians has threatened the integrity of your command. Our forces are confused and demoralized."

"Your point is well taken, Exedore. They are accustomed to decisive victories."

"I fear that this game of 'cat-and-mouse' will undermine us, my lord."

"Then perhaps the time has come to talk to them."

"I agree, Commander."

"All right then, consider it done." Breetai grinned. "But we must be persuasive. I doubt they will surrender one of their kind just for our asking."

A planet was centered in the main extravehicular monitor screen of the SDF-1. Even under full magnification it was impossible to discern any surface details; but that made no difference to the men and women on the bridge, who had long ago committed to memory those oceans and continents and distinctive cloud patterns. *Earth!* Darker than they knew it was due to the filters used on the giant reflector scopes, but their homeworld nonetheless. From their vantage, the planet was scarcely ten degrees from the solar disc itself, still on the far side of the sun, but there it was: visible, almost palpable.

Save for the ever-present whirls, hums, and beeps Robotechnology contributed to life on the bridge, you could have heard the proverbial pin drop. Lisa Hayes, Claudia Grant, Sammie, Vanessa, Kim, and Captain Gloval—all of them were transfixed by the sight. But their silence was purposeful as well as ceremonious.

They had just directed a radio beam transmission to the United Earth Defense Council headquarters and were now awaiting the response.

All at once static crackled through the overhead speakers; all eyes fixed on these now, the forward screen forgotten.

"Captain Gloval," the voice began, "due to the possibility that our security may be breached and this transmission intercepted by the enemy, we cannot give you the information you requested about our present support systems... Fortunately for us, the enemy forces were more interested in following the SDF-1, and consequently, you are requested to continue to keep them at bay and *not* return to Earth. Repeat: Do not attempt a return at this time. That is all."

This time the bridge crew was just too stunned to speak.

Finally, Vanessa deadpanned, "Welcome home."

"I can't believe this," said Claudia. "We're expected to stay out here and be sitting ducks while they, they— Oh, forgive me, sir, I've spoken out of turn."

Captain Gloval said nothing. Was it possible, he was wondering, that after more than a year in space the SDF-1 could simply be turned away, that the council had decided to offer them up as sacrifices? Gloval pressed the palms of his hands to his face as if to wipe away what his expression might betray. It was more than possible, it was probable.

Eleven years ago, when initial exploration of the recently arrived SDF-1 had revealed the remains of alien giants, the World Unification Alliance had decided to reconstruct the ship and to develop new weaponry designed for defense against this potential enemy. It was a ruse, but it had succeeded to some degree in reuniting the planet. Confrontations during the past year had made it plain to Gloval that the enemy had traveled to Earth to reclaim their ship. Just what was so important about this particular vessel remained a mystery, but it was obvious that the aliens wanted it back undamaged. The spacefold undertaken on that fateful day had inadvertently rescued Earth from any further devastation. In this way, the Robotechnicians had done their job: An alien attack had been averted.

Gloval was now forced to take a long hard look at the present situation through the eyes of the Earth leaders. And through the eyes of the enemy. Several possibilities presented themselves. The fate of the Earth might still hang in the balance regardless of whether or not the SDF-1 was captured, destroyed, or surrendered. If the Council was thinking along those lines, then perhaps work was under way on some unimaginable weapons defense system, and time was what they needed most— time that the SDF-1 could buy for them. But if the ship was the enemy's central concern, it would occur to the aliens sooner or later to use their superior firepower to hold the Earth hostage. And how could one compare the loss of 50,000 lives to the annihilation of an entire planet?

Sadly, there was something about the short message that led Gloval to believe that Earth had already written them off.

When the Captain looked up, he realized that Lisa, Claudia, and the others were staring at him, waiting for his reaction.

Full of false confidence, he stood up and said:
"We're changing course."

The Zentraedi had grown so accustomed to the Micronians' erratic behavior and unpredictability that it hardly surprised them when the SDF-1 repositioned itself. Where at one time they would have puzzled over the situation and analyzed its strategic implications, they now simply altered their plans accordingly. And it just so happened in this instance that the course change was easy to accommodate.

Breetai and Exedore communicated their attack plan to Grel, acting liaison officer for the Botoru's Seventh Division—Breetai refused to have any further direct dealings with Khyron. Grel relayed the information to his commander.

Khyron received him in his quarters onboard the battle cruiser. He had been using the dried leaves again, a habit he turned to in tranquil times, and ingested one as Grel spoke.

"They've changed course?"

"Yes, my lord. Already they have recrossed the orbit of the fourth planet, and our course projections show them closing on the system's planetoid belt."

"Hmm, yes, they seem to fear deep space. Go on."

"While the Noshiran and Harmesta assault groups are engaging the enemy, we are to choose a planetoid of suitable makeup and sufficient size and destroy it. It is Commander Breetai's belief that the Micronians will raise their shields against the resultant debris—"

"Shunting power for the shields from their main battery weapons system."

"Such is Breetai's belief. With their main gun inoperable and their Battloids engaged, Zor's ship will be rendered helpless."

Khyron slapped the table. "Then we move in for the kill!"

"No, Commander."

"What then?"

"Warning shots across the bow of the ship."

'What!—without hitting them?"

"Commander Breetai will then demand a surrender."

A look of disbelief flashed across the Khyron's face. He threw back his head and laughed. "This reeks of Exedore's hand. What can he be thinking of? We've chased these Micronians through this entire star system. They know we won't destroy the ship, so why expect a surrender now?" Khyron's gestures punctuated his words. "A demand must be backed up with the threat of annihilation."

"I agree, Commander. The Micronians have demonstrated a remarkable tenacity. They will continue to fight."

Khyron thought for a moment. "Suppose they had to fight blindfolded, Grel. Say, without their radar . . ."

"But Commander, our orders—"

"To hell with our *orders*! I'm not afraid of Breetai."

Khyron stood up and approached his underling conspiratorily.

"What we need now is someone to toss to Central Command. Someone willing to admit to a tactical blunder—a misdirected laser bolt."

"I understand, my lord."

"Good. If no one volunteers, then use your discretion and choose one . . . We must take care to cover our tracks, my dear Grel."

*   *   *

Had Lieutenant Rick Hunter been privy to Captain Gloval's decision to alter the SDF-1's course (or had he been able to read the stars), he might not have been feeling so desperate, sitting there on a bench in Macross Central Park waiting for Minmei to show. But the way Rick had figured it, Earth was only a few months away, and he had to win Minmei before they arrived. For all its 50,000 inhabitants, Macross still felt like a small town; he stood a chance here. Once they were home it would be a different story.

Rick was not in the best of moods in any case. He was still burning from his most recent confrontation with Flight Officer Lisa Hayes, and now Minmei had kept him waiting for over an hour. He checked his wristwatch against Macross City's new midday sun. A little more magic from the EVE engineers and no one was going to care about returning to Earth, he said to himself.

Since the Miss Macross pageant, Minmei had been all but inaccessible; seeing her practically required a formal appointment, and on those rare occasions when Rick managed to cut through the red tape, their time together had been brief and awkward. She hadn't even bothered to visit him in sick bay after the recon encounter. Still, the field was clear; she wasn't dating anyone. Her picture adorned the radomes of many of the Veritechs, but only Rick Hunter had access to the real thing.

He checked his watch again and looked around the park. The three bridge bunnies were approaching him. Kim, Vanessa, and . . . he couldn't remember the young one's name. He didn't feel up to making small talk with them, but there was nowhere to hide.

They started right in on him:

"Well, hello there, Lieutenant Hunter."

"Who are you waiting for?"

"Do you have a date?"

"Been waiting long?"

"Is she really beautiful?"

"Prettier than we are?" the young one asked.

Rick took a good look at them as they struck mock poses for his benefit. They were all attractive, especially the brunette in shorts. But in his eyes Minmei had them beat. He gracefully sidestepped their further questions and a moment later was rescued by a robo-phone that was cruising around the park paging him. The persistent machine was arguing with someone on a neighboring bench when Rick called out to it. Once, then again and again, adding volume to each shout.

Finally the phone homed in on him, insulting some innocent as it left the nearby bench. Rick deposited a coin; Minmei's face appeared in the viewscreen. The three women moved behind him to get a better look. Rick didn't hear their surprised reactions at seeing Miss Macross on the screen and barely acknowledged their good-byes when they wandered off.

Minmei was apologizing. ". . . It's just that my singing lesson was set back an hour and I'm afraid I'm not going to make it now."

"That's great, Minmei. The one afternoon I'm not on flight duty and you've got singing lessons."

"Listen, Rick, they've decided to do a recording session—"

"Another new career for the 'Queen'?"

Minmei's response was interrupted. She turned away from the camera to respond to someone seated at a piano. The guy was summoning her back to practice.

Minmei said, "Rick, I've got to go," and broke the line.

The robophone moved off. Rick took a walk through the park, not sure if he was feeling anger or self-pity. He was standing by the central fountain when the city's warning sirens sounded. A general alert, but conditional, not confrontational—an environmental threat as opposed to an enemy attack. People were heading toward shelters, but with such unconcern that Rick was tempted to ride it out where he stood.

But just then the fortress was struck.

Rick was knocked off his feet and thrown into the fountain—that fountain that figured all too frequently in his thoughts of fond moments and better times. But he had no time to bathe in waves of memory or irony. The ship was sustaining impact after impact, shaking Macross City to its foundations, and the mood was now one of panic. The "sun" disappeared, and through the overhead starlight, Rick could see an enormous hunk of planetary debris on a collision course with the ship.

"Sound general quarters!" ordered Gloval as he stooped to retrieve his cap. "Give me course correction options based on the current data, and alert—"

The bridge quaked with such force that Gloval was thrown from his chair. Fragments of the exploded asteroid Pamir continued their rain of death against the ship. Klaxons blared, and damage reports poured in.

"Our port side is taking the brunt of it, sir," said Lisa. "Macross is being badly shaken."

"All right," Gloval said, picking himself up. "Concentrate the shield energy there. Divert weapons power to the pin-point barrier system. And get me the air wing commander."

"I have Skull Leader on the horn," said Claudia. "He

reports heavy fighting in the Third Quadrant. He's requesting backup, Commander."

"Negative. Give him the situation here. Tell him to stand by for recall. In a minute we're going to be defenseless."

Vanessa, Sammie, and Kim stumbled onto the bridge as Gloval was issuing course correction coordinates. The three women strapped in and began to monitor ship systems status.

It was Vanessa's threat board that revealed the enemy ships.

"Enemy destroyers! They're moving into firing position."

"Those bastards!" yelled Gloval. "Reroute power to the main gun."

"Sir, Macross City will be destroyed if we lower the shields," said Sammie.

"You have your orders," Claudia reminded the young tech. "Without defenses there won't *be* any Macross City!"

"Confirm enemy fire—laser-bolt signatures!"

"Brace yourselves!" said Gloval.

But no shock came. The SDF-1 was fenced in by blue lightning but left unstruck. And Gloval didn't know what to make of it. All at once, however, it became a moot point: The ship sustained a terrible direct hit. All systems failed on the bridge. Presently auxiliary power brought some of them back to life. Gloval requested damage assessment from all stations.

Lisa reported the worst news: The conning tower had been hit. The entire radar control crew had been wiped out.

Gloval ordered all engines stopped.

The dimensional fortress shut down. The enemy had

ceased their fire, but chunks of rock continued to impact against it. Debris from the conning tower drifted by the front and side bays. Lisa averted her gaze from the sight of a human body hanging lifeless in the void, a red-trimmed Battloid . . .

"Can we raise Skull Leader?"

"Negative, sir," said Claudia.

"Do we have any radar functioning—wide-range, perhaps?"

"The report from the technical repair unit is coming in now," said Lisa. She listened a moment. "Estimates of ten hours to effect minimal repairs."

Gloval said nothing; his silence was unnerving to the rest of them.

Incoming data to Sammie's station broke the stalemate. It registered as code, but unlike any encrypted transmissions they were familiar with. Gloval ordered her to patch it through the speakers. The ever-present static of deep space infiltrated the bridge; then, a voice: deep, resonant, menacing.

"In the name of the Zentraedi forces, I order you to surrender. The last attack on your ship was a warning of what we will do. You cannot escape. If you wish to save the lives of your crew, you must surrender at once."

"My God," said Claudia. "It's the aliens!"

"We repeat," the voice continued, "in the name of the Zentraedi forces, I order you to surrender. The last attack on your ship . . ."

Gloval listened carefully to the message. The *Zentraedi*, he said to himself.

Now at least he knew what to call them.

CHAPTER
TWELVE

It was only during the final stages of the [Global] War that women were assigned to active military operations. Up until that time most women held rear-echelon positions; but as casualties increased among the men unilaterally, these positions came to be of paramount importance. Indeed, by the time of the First Robotech War those positions could only be filled by women. True, there were no women on the United Earth Council, but the entire bridge crew of the super dimensional fortress, the SDF-1, was female. One recalls the postfeminist claims that women were now not only victimized by male aggressive instincts but instrumental in carrying them out, that women (especially in the case of the SDF-1) had exchanged the traditional pots and pans for the keyboards and consoles of the bridge. But those claims not only simplify the issue but malign those women who contributed their unique skills to the war effort. What is most disconcerting is the fact that although women had finally achieved their long-sought-after goal of equality, the Global War had introduced a new set of polarizing issues which now had to be taken into account—there was mutual respect between the sexes but a continued sense of the same old bugaboo about knowing and adhering to "one's place in the world." In terms of male-female relationships, the attitudes of twenty-first-century society suggested those prevalent in the middle of the previous century.

Betty Greer, *Post-Feminism and the Global War*

THE CAT'S-EYE RECON UNIT, ESCORTED BY RICK Hunter's Vermilion Team, was launched from the flight deck of the *Prometheus*. Fragments of the exploded planetoid littered local space.

Where only hours before they had been ordered to buy time for the United Earth Defense Council, Captain Gloval was now buying time for the SDF-1. The enemy's offensive strength had to be ascertained—the *Zentraedi's* strength—and with the ship's radar down this could be achieved only by deploying the recon vessel.

Lisa Hayes had the stick—the unit's former pilot had been a casualty in the latest Zentraedi offensive. Her copilot was an inexperienced second lieutenant on loan from the Gladiator Defense Force. Most of the air wing strike teams had been deployed to guard the badly damaged SDF-1, looking crippled and deathly still now on the Cat's-Eye's rear commo screen.

Lieutenant Hunter was on the forward screen.

"Ironic, isn't it, Commander," he was saying, "that I should end up your wingman?"

Lisa knew what he was referring to; less than twenty-four hours ago they had gotten into yet another tiff.

One of Vermilion squadron's VTs had taken a hit, and Hunter had informed the bridge that he was taking his group home. The pilot of the stricken VT maintained that the damage was only slight, and scanners showed continued fighting in Hunter's quadrant, with only the Skull Team left to take up the slack; so Lisa had denied him permission to come in.

"I'll be the judge of that," Hunter had said. "I'm group leader, and I'm responsible for the safety of my men!" Then he went on to lecture her about the dynamics of space dogfighting, how seemingly insignificant damage could quickly prove fatal, how she was safe and sound on the bridge while the big brave men of the VT strike force were constantly in jeopardy...On and on.

She dismissed it as battle fatigue. But instead of letting it go, she had vented her own anger and frustration. After all, she *was* his superior.

Then Roy Fokker, guitar-strumming darling of the Defense Force, had stepped in on Hunter's side. They went right into their big brother–little brother act, and the next thing Lisa knew, Fokker was ordering the Vermilion Team home. He did, however, scold Hunter for talking too much.

If the incident had ended there, she would have forgotten it by now. But among the space debris that had floated past the bridge bays following the Zentraedi attack there was a disabled Battloid she had been certain was Hunter's red-trimmed own. She had even imagined (or, more likely, hallucinated) that she saw Rick's lifeless form drift from the shattered cockpit module . . .

Even now the image was too painful to recall.

Hunter had rescued her on Mars. But so what? He'd been *ordered* to do it. Any of the VT pilots would have done so; it certainly didn't mean that she had to feel anything special for the guy. Of course, it might have been different if she felt something coming from him, but—

"I show four bogies at four o'clock relative," her copilot informed her.

"I see them," Lisa heard Rick say.

"There going to try a surprise attack," said Ben Dixon. "Let me at 'em."

"Negative, Ben," Hunter countered. "Do not give pursuit. We're going to stick to the Eye."

Here he goes, thought Lisa. He was doing it again, making her feel like she couldn't take care of herself. He infuriated her with his unsolicited protection. She went on the tac net.

"I can protect myself, Lieutenant Hunter. Give pursuit. That's a direct order, do you copy?"

Hunter was silent for a moment, then said, "All right, boys, you heard the little woman. Let's go get 'em."

The three VTs of Vermilion Team broke formation and went after the Battlepods. The Cat's-Eye was relaying positional data to them, but the enemy bandits were still too far off for visual contact. Rick called up full magnification on his port and starboard screens, and suddenly there they were: guns bristling, extended claw thrusters radiant in the perpetual night.

"I see them," said Max Sterling. "Going in . . ."

Max and Ben, both of them anxious to post a few more pod decals on their fighters, hit their afterburners and passed Rick by. Rick found himself holding back, thinking about Lisa's safety. *Damn her*, he thought. *Let her go ahead and get herself atomized.* What did he care? He shook his head as if to clear it and threw his VT into the fight.

A Battlepod had swooped in and fixed him in its lasers. Rick in turn engaged his starboard thrusters, then cut his forward speed and fell away from the laser lock. At the same time, he loosed aft heat-seekers, which caught the pod where the legs met the spherical body. The pods were highly vulnerable there, and this one went into an uncontrolled accelerated spin as the legs blew away. Rick saw two quick flashes ahead of him, and soon his fighter was sailing through more pod debris.

It was easy if you let yourself think of the pods themselves as the enemy. Remind yourself that there was a fifty-foot humanoid giant in each of them though, and your brain began to short-circuit. In Battloid mode, Rick had been face to face with Zentraedi warriors on two occasions. And each time he had been paralyzed with fear. The Robotech Defenders who had trained on Earth before the invasion had been shown the skeletons and had been conditioned to *accept* the reality, but Rick had to learn it the hard way. Rick, however, was one of the few men who had actually met a live Zentraedi and lived to tell about it.

Battloids were the perfect mating of mind and mecha and were ideally suited to a war with giants. But what would it be like to confront a Zentraedi without the mecha? What could you do against something ten times your size? There was a seventy-year-old film on video-tape in the ship's library about a giant ape who had been found on a remote Pacific island. The ape had terrorized New York City the way later mutants and giants would wreak havoc on Tokyo. But there was something about that old film...it had somehow managed to communicate the mixture of awe and terror Rick felt when he faced the giants. There had been a woman in that film, he recalled...

The Battlepods destroyed, he switched on the tac net and tried to raise the Cat's-Eye. But there was no response.

The recon ship was in trouble.

In pursuit of their surveillance mission, Lisa and her copilot had entered into an area filled with massive chunks of what had once been the planetoid Pamir. They had their hands full dodging these while at the same time reporting on enemy locations.

"We have multiple radar contacts, picking up four, five, six, eight, and twelve heavy," the copilot said.

Lisa watched the radar hand sweep across the color-enhanced screen. There was something enormous ahead of them. It would have to measure more than fifteen kilometers in length. Possibly a piece of Pamir, but the shape was all wrong. This thing was like an elongated ellipse, a zero stretched at its poles. It had to be an enemy ship!

She began maneuvering the Cat's-Eye in for a closer look, her attention fixed on the radar screen.

She didn't see the island of space rock they collided with.

The radar disc was torn from the ship, and one by one the life support systems began to fail. The forward portion of the canopy was damaged but intact. But the copilot had not been as fortunate; his limp form hung in space, still tethered to the ship by an untorn length of seat strap. *There's no atmosphere in space*, Hunter's words came back to her before she slipped from consciousness.

The smallest damage could prove fatal.

Exedore watched his commander pace the bridge.

Continuous setbacks and defeats at the hands of the Micronians were beginning to take their toll.

When the projecbeam field formed itself for viewing, the now crippled SDF-1 could be discerned amid the asteroid field. Scanners indicated that Micronian fighters had taken up defensive positions in all quadrants in anticipation of a second offensive.

"Look at that ship," said Breetai. "We're fortunate that it survived the attack."

"No thanks to Khyron. This time he has gone too far."

"Too far, indeed. And do you see how the Micronians react to our demands for surrender, Exedore? They ignore us."

"Yes, Commander. I fear that they have seen through our strategy. There is in fact a word for it in their language—bluff. It means to mislead or intimidate through pretense."

The comlink tone sounded on the bridge, followed by the voice of the duty officer.

"Commander Breetai, we have Commander Khyron standing by."

Breetai dissolved the projecbeam and hit the communicator switch. "Patch him through—immediately!"

Khyron wore his familiar expression of slight bemusement. Exedore had heard rumors to the effect that he was addicted to the Invid Flower; if this was true, Khyron was even more dangerous than Breetai realized.

"You will be pleased to learn that the matter has already been settled," the Backstabber was saying.

A frightened junior officer was then shoved forward into the screen's field of view. His shackled hands managed a two-handed breast salute as Khyron ordered him to speak.

"Commander Breetai, I take full responsibility for the misplaced laser bolt which destroyed the radar tower of Zor's ship. My aim was untrue, and I humbly await your judgment."

The officer hung his head in shame.

Breetai stared at the screen with a look of disbelief that quickly refocused as anger.

"Khyron, do you take me for a complete fool?!"

Khyron smirked, "Not complete, Breetai."

Exedore's commander was enraged; he shouted, "You have not heard the end of this!" and shut down the comlink. He resumed his pacing as a second message was fed to the bridge: An enemy recon vessel disabled by a collision with an asteroid had been captured and was being brought to the flagship.

So something had been salvaged from this operation,

after all, Breetai told himself. He heard Exedore give the order that all survivors were to be left unharmed.

"Well, Exedore, it looks like you'll have the specimens you wanted."

"So it would appear, Commander," Exedore replied guardedly. These would-be minor triumphs had a vexing way of reversing themselves.

Nevertheless, Exedore and Breetai rushed from the bridge and made for the docking bays. They were halfway along the main corridor to the elevators when an announcement from ship security brought them to a halt.

"Three Micronian ships in pursuit of the captured recon craft have broken into the lower deck holding area. Commander Breetai, contact the bridge."

Breetai growled, "They *dare* to enter my ship?! Now I will deal with them *personally*!"

The Zentraedi commander broke into a run; Exedore was behind him, throwing caution to the wind.

The Vermilion Team had pursued the captured Cat's-Eye into the lower hold of the huge ship, reconfiguring to Guardian mode when they cleared the hatchway. Afterburners were now accelerating them along the kilometers of floor in the enormous chamber.

Rick took out the enemy tow which had ensnared Lisa's craft and ordered the team into Battloid configuration. The two Zentraedi pilots who jumped from the flaming wreck were easily chased off by gatling fire loosed by Max and Ben.

The two corporals were speechless. Those were living, breathing *giants* who had clambered out of the tow. All that training—the photos, the videos, the skeletal remains—hadn't prepared them for this moment of actual confrontation. They couldn't help but notice, how ever, that the place was a wreck all on its own: Spare parts from Battlepods and other mecha littered the area, overhead gantries and hull hatchways were in desperate need of attention, and an atmosphere of ultimate neglect and disrepair hung over the area like the stench of decay.

Rick, meanwhile, was bringing the Battloid down on one knee to inspect the Cat's-Eye. He could see Lisa begin to stir inside the smashed cockpit. Seeing the Battloid, she switched on the external speakers.

"Lieutenant Hunter, take your men and get out of here. You've got no time to spare."

Her voice was weak.

"Time enough to bring you with us."

Max came on the line: "Lieutenant, the Zentraedi are taking up positions at the end of the corridor. We better blow this place."

"Just give me a few minutes of cover fire, Max. Then we're outta here."

"That'll just about deplete my cannon charge."

"Mine, too," Ben added.

"Cut the chatter. Open fire."

Rick returned his attention to the Cat's-Eye while his teammates laid down a deafening barrage of fire.

"Can you operate the manual eject mechanism, Commander?"

"Negative," Lisa answered him. "The controls are jammed. Move out, Lieutenant. I'm giving you an order."

"This is no time to stand on protocol, Commander. Cover yourself; I'm going to break into the cockpit."

Lisa saw the Battloid's enormous hand come down on the shield and screamed, "Keep your hand off me, Hunter! I'm not kidding, don't touch me with that thing!"

The Battloid's fingers pinched the shield, shattering it. Cursing Rick the entire while, Lisa pulled herself up and free of the wreckage.

"I'll have your stripes for this, Hunter. I swear it."

Rick heard Ben's gatling sputter out; Max flashed him a signal that he, too, was out of ammo. Lisa had moved away from the Cat's-Eye. Rick was offering her the outstretched open hand of the Battloid when he caught her startled reaction to something that had appeared on the overhead catwalk.

Halfway to standing, that something landed *hard* on the Battloid's back, driving the mecha to the floor of the hold with a force not to be believed.

CHAPTER
THIRTEEN

Few of us were fortunate enough to have seen the interior of the SDF-1 before Dr. Lang's teams of Robotechnicians had retrofit the fortress with bulkheads, partitions, lowered ceilings, and doorways and hatches proportioned to human scale; so our entry into the enormous lower hold of [Breetai's] flagship proved to be a veritable assault on the senses. Although I learned much later that human-size enclosures did in fact exist aboard the SDF-1 prior to reconstruction, here were all the things Sterling, Dixon, and I had been hearing about from members of the early exploratory teams: the three-hundred-foot-high ceilings, thirty-foot-wide hatchways, miles of corridors ... It was not surprising, then, that our minds refused to grapple with these new dimensions. We didn't experience the hold as human beings entering giant-sized spaces; it was instead as if we had been reduced in size!

The Collected Journals of Admiral Rick Hunter

EVEN BY ZENTRAEDI STANDARDS, THE SOLDIER WHO leapt from the hold gantry and decked Rick Hunter's Battloid was enormous.

Max calculated the giant's height at sixty-plus feet. He wore knee-high utility boots and a blue uniform trimmed in yellow at the collar and sleeves; over this was a long, sleeveless brown tunic adorned with one bold vertical blue band. At breast level was some sort of insignia or badge of rank—almost a black musical note in a yellow field. But the most memorable thing about him was the gleaming plate that covered one side of his head, inset with what appeared to be a lusterless cabochon. He had jumped more than 200 feet from the catwalk, yet here he stood glaring at them, ready to take on the entire Robotech Defense Force single-handed.

Max didn't have to be told that he'd met one of the Zentraedi elite.

Sterling allowed these diverse emotional reactions to wash through him; he then relaxed and began to attune his thoughts to the Battloid's capabilities. Quickly positioning his mecha behind the giant, he swung the depleted gatling cannon across the warrior's chest and held it fast with both hands, pinioning the giant's arms at his sides. Displays in the Battloid cockpit module ran wild as the Zentraedi struggled to free himself. Max could sense the extent of the enemy's will reaching into his own mind and grappling with it on some newly opened front in this war, a psycho-battleground.

The Battloid's arms were stressed to the limit, threatening to dislocate with each of the giant's chest expansions. The Zentraedi was growling like a trapped animal, twisting his head around, each deliberate move calculated to bring that gleaming faceplate into violent contact with the canopy of the mecha. Max knew that something was going to give out soon unless he changed tactics.

The Battloid's environmental sensors indicated that the hold was indeed an air lock; it could therefore be depressurized. Max wasn't certain what size hole would be necessary to achieve the effect he was after, but he had to take a chance. He raised Ben on the tac net, all the while struggling with foot pedals and random thoughts, and ordered him to fire his warheads at the ship's hull directly overhead.

Ben triggered release of the missiles; the explosion

tore a gaping hole in the ship. But something unexpected was happening even before the smoke was sucked clear: The hull was actually repairing itself! Max couldn't believe his sensors; the process was almost organic, as though the ship was . . . alive.

But he lost no time thinking about it. He fired the mecha's foot thrusters, launching himself, along with the Zentraedi, toward the ceiling. Just short of the healing rend, he released his grip on the cannon. Momentum carried the giant out into space seconds before the hull patch completed itself.

Back on the floor of the hold, Rick had picked himself up. He had snatched Lisa from midair during the depressurization and was holding her in the Battloid's metal-shod hand now, ignoring her protestations. Max brought his Battloid down beside him.

"Nice work, Max. Guess we won't be seeing that character again."

"Not unless he can survive deep space without an extravehicular suit."

"Now what do we do?" Ben asked.

The three men panned their Battloid video cameras across the hold, searching for a way out.

Breetai, meanwhile, who was made of much sterner stuff than any of the Earthlings realized, was not only alive but was at that moment pulling his way along the outer skin of the flagship, using as handholds the numerous sensor bristles and antennae that covered the ship. The gaping hole had of course closed itself too quickly to permit reentry into the hold, but he had managed to recollect his strength by latching on to a jagged piece of the ruptured hull before beginning his trek across the exterior armor plating.

His genetic makeup allowed him to withstand the vacuum of deep space for a limited period only, but he had nothing less than complete confidence in his ability to survive. Thoughts of vengeance drove him on: That Micronian was going to pay dearly for this.

Inside the ship, the diminutive Lisa Hayes had resumed command of the three pilots in their Battloids. She spoke into her helmet communicator from the open hand of Rick Hunter's mecha, instructing Max and Ben to use their top-mounted lasers to burn through the port hatch.

"You'll have to do it quickly," she advised them. "They're going to be on us any second now." She then swung herself around to face Rick. "And Lieutenant, would you mind putting me down now? I know how you enjoy holding me, but you'll have to learn to admire me from a distance."

Rick mumbled something into his headset and set his commander back on the floor of the hold. Max and Ben were taking alternate turns on the air lock to keep their lasers from overheating.

Rick stepped forward to join them. He was motioning Ben's Battloid aside when he heard what sounded like a war cry—not through his headset but shattering the air of the hold itself. He spun the Battloid around in time to see the returned Zentraedi leap from an open hatchway overhead. The giant attacked like a samurai warrior; he held aloft a thick, pipelike tool that he brought down with gargantuan strength on the head of Ben's Battloid, dropping the mecha to the floor with a resounding crash.

The Zentraedi stood victorious over his fallen enemy, then turned his attention to Max and Rick. Issuing a guttural sound, he gripped the tool with both hands and thrust it in front of him.

Max and Rick separated some and raised their useless

cannons, gripping them palms down like battle staffs.
The Zentraedi was moving in slowly, each step calculated and deliberate.

"He's getting ready to charge," said Max.

Rick risked a step forward, motioning Max to fall in
behind him. He brought the cannon up over his head and
stood his ground, waiting for the charge.

The Zentraedi launched himself with a basso yell.
Rick planted himself and brought the cannon down like a
sledge, putting every ounce of strength he could summon
into the blow. Metal met metal with fusion force.

Breetai swung his weapon like a bat, sending the gatling flying from the Battloid's hands. it hit the floor nose
first, almost flattening Lisa Hayes.

Now six more Zentraedi soldiers in helmets and full-
body armor arrived on the scene. One of them rushed
forward with some sort of satchel and sacked the dazed
Micronian pilot.

Max witnessed it, but three soldiers now stood between him and the commander. Regardless, he moved in
to engage one of them. The Zentraedi tried to wrestle the
gatling from his grip, so Max turned the sallow-faced
man's strength to his own advantage, relaxing his own
hold on the cannon for a moment, then using the soldier's uncontrolled momentum to heave him to the floor.
But he was hardly in the clear: A cluster of five more
were opening fire on him with shock guns. Max tossed
aside the cannon and leaped up, firing the Battloid foot
thrusters as he did so. Halfway to the ceiling of the hold
he reached for the mode levers, reconfigured the Guardian, and began returning fire, dodging blue bolts of energy that shot past him and impacted on the inner skin of
the ship.

Rick had been knocked flat on his back by the Zentraedi commander. The giant stood over him now, preparing to pile-drive the tool through the Battloid's abdomen. Rick brought the mecha's right leg up, bent at the knee, and fired the foot thruster full into the face of his assailant. As the Zentraedi went back, clutching his face and losing his grip on the weapon, Rick pulled his thruster lever home and went in for the kill, catching the giant's midsection and somersaulting him into a midair front flip. But the giant somehow managed to reverse the throw. Although Rick landed on top of him, he found himself facing the Zentraedi's feet. And the next thing he knew, he was being pressed into the air by the standing Zentraedi and launched across the hold.

Rick engaged the shoulder retros to cut his airspeed. He executed a neat front flip with a half twist that left him standing face to face with the Zentraedi, but he was unfortunately off balance and stunned. A right cross followed by a front kick sent him down to the floor again. This time his opponent was playing for keeps.

Breetai grabbed the mecha by its right arm, spun it into a three-sixty, and hurled it against a set of bulkhead cargo spikes; these perforated the Battloid's arms, chest, and shoulders and left it hanging there, pinned to the wall.

Identifying with the mecha, Rick felt like the victim of a careless circus knife thrower. The Battloid was immobilized, half its systems disabled, and now this giant with the faceplate was coming in to finish him off. Valiantly, Rick fired the top-mounted lasers, but the Zentraedi dropped himself out of range in the nick of time.

Rick was suddenly looking at foot-long life and love lines—the giant had brought his hand up over the canopy and was beginning to crush it. One by one the life support systems began to fail. And now the giant was working on the chestplates, literally tearing the Battloid apart! He ripped the armor from the mecha and tossed it aside as though it weighed nothing.

Grinning, the Zentraedi peered in at him now through the torn cockpit module, taking obvious delight in Rick's fearful situation. Rick, armed the mecha's still-functioning self-destruct warhead and in desperation, reached down under the seat for the manual-eject ring and gave it a wholehearted tug. The head of the Battloid lolled forward, its explosive charges crippled, but the cockpit seat managed to launch itself.

The Zentraedi, too, launched himself with a powerful jump. He snatched Rick from the air, crushing him in his fist, bringing on blessed relief from further fear...

Witnessing the giant's catch, Max, his Guardian still moving through the hold dodging laser bolts, was certain that the lieutenant had been killed. Hunter's murderer was going to pay in kind, Max decided. He nose-dived the VT, preparing to loose all the firepower he had left.

But all at once the remains of Rick's Battloid exploded. The Zentraedi was thrown off his feet, a breach was blown in the hull, and Max's Veritech was sucked from the air lock.

The hull quickly sealed itself, and the Zentraedi soldiers gathered around their fallen commander. Breetai was flat out on his back, his tunic and uniform torn and tattered. But he was made of sterner stuff than even *they* realized. He said as much as he got up.

His right hand was still clenched. Carefully he relaxed his grip to regard the small creature held there, strapped to its ejection seat, unmoving and as quiet as death.

CHAPTER
FOURTEEN

As I have elsewhere stated, preliminary tests on the three Micronian subjects indicate that their anatomical makeup and physiological systems are very similar to those of the Zentraedi; I hasten to add, however, that I am here referring to "wet-state" subjects rather than mature and viable ones. [Editor's note: There is as yet no adequate Panglish equivalent of the Zentraedi term. Some linguistic camps favor "pretransformized," while others have pushed for "neocast" or "neocloned." See Kazinsky, Chapters Seven and Eight, for a lively overview of the continuing controversy.] Subsequent psychoscanning, in any case, brought to light the dissimilarities which are the focus of this report. These include: (1) significant anomalies throughout the neocortical regions and topical convolutionary conduits, (2) structural anomalies in the vascular and neural networks of the infundibulum, the pyramidal tracts, and the hippocampus, (3) pineal insufficiency, and (4) reticular imbalance of the pons and attendant cerebellar pathways.

Exedore, from his Military Intelligence Analysis Reports to the Zentraedi High Command

Micronians think too much!

Khyron

PREVIOUS DEALINGS WITH MICRONIANS HAD LARGE-ly been a matter of eradication. But now Exedore actually had three live specimens to analyze and examine. And the results of tests thus far conducted were as surprising as they were baffling and discomforting. Genetically, anatomically, and physiologically, the Micronians appeared to be almost identical to the Zentraedi. They were of course culturally and behavioristically worlds apart, but the physical similarities suggested a point of common origin lost to time and history.

Exedore studied the prisoners from his sealed-off operating station inside the ship's laboratory—who knew what contagious diseases these beings harbored? The scanner umbrella which in effect kept them isolated and confined to the specimen table was probably sufficient in itself for this, but Exedore was taking no chances.

Breetai, however, wanted no part of the laboratory or the operating station. Exedore brought him up to date on the findings in the command center, illustrating facts and speculations with data readouts, x-rays, scans of various sorts, and relevant historical documents, all of which flowed freely across the center's many monitor screens.

Breetai took particular interest in the female of the group. He shifted his attention from one screen's anatomical depictions and turned to the specimen table monitor. The Micronian female appeared to be unconscious or asleep, the other two as well.

"Is it wise to keep the female and males together?"

Exedore had the camera close on the table. "It is apparently their practice, Commander. It will certainly benefit us to observe their interactions."

A look of surprise came over Breetai's face, and Exedore now turned his attention to the monitor. The Micronians were beginning to stir.

The two Zentraedi watched intently.

The black-haired one was first to rise—the tough little pilot who had manned the mecha Breetai had destroyed. The female recon pilot was next, but together they couldn't seem to rouse the third and largest member of their party.

"This one has a very slow metabolic rate and is less intelligent than the others," Exedore said by way of explanation.

Something curious began to happen just then: The female and the male were arguing. Breetai signaled his adviser to activate the audio monitors. The words came fast and furious and were for the most part unfamiliar to Breetai, but he understood enough to get the gist: They were blaming each other for the failure of their mission and their eventual capture.

Breetai was amused.

"They fight with words as aggressively as they fight with mecha."

"A result of the commingling of males and females, sir—an ancient practice long ago abandoned by the Zentraedi."

"I see . . . anger without discipline."

"Precisely that, Commander."

As Breetai continued to observe the argument, however, he was overcome by a feeling of sickness; he felt debilitated and phobic. He ordered Exedore to deactivate the monitor and collapsed down into his chair.

"My head is spinning. I can no longer stand to watch them."

"I feel the same," said Exedore. "However, we must not allow any of our personal reactions to interfere with the mission at hand."

Breetai lifted up his head. "Well, suppose you tell me how I should proceed with these creatures."

"The Micronians should be brought to Dolza himself. There they should be subjected to the most rigorous interrogation possible."

"That will require a fold operation and the expenditure of substantial quantities of energy."

"It will be justified, Commander. The Micronians' own words will doom them to defeat."

Lisa couldn't believe her ears: Who in the known universe did Hunter think he was talking to?

She and Hunter and dead-to-the-world Dixon were on some sort of alien grid platform, curtained and contained by a nebulous rain of electrical energy directed from an overhead generator. But through this translucent umbrella could be glimpsed the enormous machines, scopes, scanners, and data analyzers that constituted the laboratory beyond. One portion of the energy canopy afforded them visual access to an exterior bay of the ship. And somewhere out among that starfield was the SDF-1 and a world the three of them might never see again.

Hunter, nevertheless, seemed less interested in establishing where they were than in establishing who was to blame for their being there.

"Are you telling me that you wouldn't have been captured if a *man* had been piloting the Cat's-Eye? Because if you are—"

"I'm not saying that. I'm just saying there are some jobs that are better left to experienced pilots. You don't find VT pilots muscling onto the bridge, do you?"

Lisa glared at him. "I'm your superior, Lieutenant Hunter!"

"Only in rank, *Commander* Hayes."

"In rank and military experience!"

Rick made a dismissive gesture. "Don't give me that Robotech Academy superiority. I'm talking about *combat* experience."

Lisa crossed her arms to keep him from noticing that she was shaking with anger. Her foot tapped reflexively.

"Do you need to be reminded of the *conversation* we had yesterday—the one where you complained about my always being 'safe and sound on the bridge'? Now I'm out here with you, and I still can't do anything right in your eyes. It's a no-win situation with you, mister."

Rick softened somewhat. "Look, it's just that I feel more...I don't know, *vulnerable*, with you around. You're always getting yourself in a fix, just like on Sara Base—"

"Hunter!" she screamed. "You're an idiot! Just who appointed you my personal guardian?"

"Someone's gotta protect you from yourself."

She looked around for something to throw at him, but Dixon would be too heavy and there was nothing else on the grid.

"Who had to be towed in after completely destroying the armored Battloid, Lieutenant?"

Rick's face went red with rage and embarrassment.

"You think fighting these Zentraedi is some kind of cakewalk? Maybe you didn't see that guy tear my mecha apart with his bare hands, huh?"

"No, I didn't see it. *I* was in the sack, remember?"

"Yeah, well..."

"Yeah, well," she mimicked him, and turned away.

Ben Dixon was coming to, stretching and yawning as though he'd just taken a terrific nap.

He looked around and asked if he had missed anything.

Rick shot Lisa a cruel look and stepped over to his corporal. "Uh, nothing much, Ben. The *Commander* and I were just discussing an escape plan."

Lisa smirked and looked out the bay.

"Great," Ben said. "When do we get started?"

Rick said something Lisa didn't catch; she was too mesmerized by what was occurring outside the ship: The stars were becoming tentative, strung out, as if trailing threads of light behind them.

My God! She realized what she was seeing. The Zentraedi were beginning a fold operation!

Back onboard the SDF-1 the period of anxious waiting had ended an hour ago with the restoration of wide-range radar. But a new period of apprehension had just begun. The bridge had lost communication with the Cat's-Eye recon and the VTs of the Vermilion Team, and now there was evidence of fluctuations in the timespace continuum of that area. Most of the massive enemy ships had disappeared from the scanner screen, but numerous small ships and battle mecha were still swirling around the fortress. Gloval was certain that half the fleet had executed a spacefold.

In all his long years of military command, Gloval had never faced a more unpredictable foe. They had crippled his ship, threatened him with extinction, demanded surrender, and suddenly disappeared off the scopes. Gloval was perplexed.

He instructed Sammie to try to raise Commander Hayes again.

"Negative response, sir. I can't raise anyone at all in that Veritech group."

Have we lost them? Gloval wondered. *Please, not Lisa!*

"Sir, we can't just give up on them," said Sammie.

"It could be radio trouble," Claudia added.

"I'm not about to give up on them," Gloval said at last. "But we can't afford to sit here and wait for the enemy to return and make good their threats." He hung his head. "We'll give them twelve hours. Claudia, if we've had no contact with them by then, I want the ship out of this quadrant by oh-six-hundred hours. Is that clear?"

"Yes, Captain. And about Commander Hayes . . . and Lieutenant Hunter and his men?"

"Enter their names on the list," Gloval responded flatly. "Missing in action and presumed dead."

Roy Fokker seldom visited Macross City, and when he did it was usually at Claudia's insistence—dinner somewhere, a movie, or the Miss Macross pageant a while back. It wasn't that he didn't like the place, just that he had little use for it. Its presence onboard the SDF-1 had all but undermined the ship's original purpose. The SDF-1 was to be Earth's guardian and defender, not surrogate or microcosm, and certainly not *decoy*. As one of the men (along with Dr. Lang and Colonel Edwards) who had first explored the ship shortly after its arrival on Earth, Fokker had a profound attachment to her. But the spacefold accident and this resulting city had devitalized that attachment, and for the past year Fokker had come to feel more the hopeless prisoner than anything else.

His motivations for visiting the city today, however, had nothing to do with entertainment or a lover's obligation; he was here because duty demanded it of him. Rick had been MIA for almost two weeks now, and there were people who had to be told.

Two weeks missing in action, Roy told himself. Was it still too early to grieve, or was it too late? Wouldn't he be able to feel the truth one way or another in his heart? Their friendship went so far back . . . Pop Hunter's flying circus, the fateful day Rick had turned up on Macross Island, their first mission together—

What was the use of tormenting himself? When he did search his heart for feelings, he found his "Little Brother" alive—this was a certainty. And yet, his mind would ask, what were the odds they would ever see each other again? The SDF-1 was a million miles from that area in space where Rick and the others had last been heard from, way beyond the range of any VT. And did it ease the pain any to think of him as a prisoner? The Zentraedi weren't likely to hold him hostage, not when they had an entire planet at their disposal. So maybe it *was* better to believe the worst, accept his death and get the grief behind him. Then he could at least remove himself from this timeless agony and begin to court the future once again.

It might have been the need for partnership in grief that led Roy to seek out Minmei. He, too, had been attracted to the blue-eyed Chinese girl from the start, and he liked to think that there was some special bond there, even though Minmei rarely acknowledged it by words or actions. But that wasn't her style, anyway. Especially now that she was on the brink of stardom. In fact, the "Queen of Macross" was going to be headlining a concert at the Star Bowl on Monday night.

Soon she was coming down the sidewalk toward him, flanked by two of her woman friends and looking the starlet part in some sort of green military-chic shorts outfit, complete with epaulets and rank stripes. Roy recognized it as the piece she'd worn for the Defense Force enlistment posters that had begun to show up all over the city.

Roy had been waiting for her outside the White Dragon. As she approached, he straightened up to his full height, tugged down on his belted jacket, and waved to her.

She came at him with a big smile, increasing her pace and excusing herself from her friends. Right off, she wanted to know if Rick was with him.

He returned the smile, strained though it was, and suggested they take a walk together. She looked at him questioningly.

"Why, Roy? What's happened?"

"Come on, walk with me a minute."

She pulled back when he tried to take her arm.

"I don't want to take a walk, Roy! What's happened? Where's Rick? Has something happened to Rick?"

Roy faced her, placing both hands on her shoulders, towering over her. He met her eyes and held them as he explained.

Halfway through his explanation she was shaking her head, refusing to believe him. "He's dead!"

"Minmei, listen, please don't think he's dead—we don't know that for sure."

Roy was doing just what he had promised himself he wouldn't do. And she was inconsolable. She twisted free of his hold.

"I don't want to hear anymore! You're a liar, and I hate you!"

She glared at him, turned, and ran off.

Her friends offered him sympathetic smiles. Roy stood with them, feeling utterly helpless. He sucked in breath and tears and clenched his teeth.

Minmei ran to *their* bench in the park.

It was a special bench, set apart from the others in Macross Central, tucked away on a small subtier of its own overhung by the full branches of an oak tree and surrounded by flowering plants and thick bushes. It was almost a secret place, curiously unfrequented by park users, with an incredible view of the city spread out below and the closest view possible through the enormous starlight in the ship's hull. Rick used to say that it was their balcony "with a view of forever."

They spent many long hours here—after their two-week ordeal together, before Rick had joined the Defense Force, and before Minmei had been crowned "Queen"... She had listened to Rick talk about the horrors of space battle, his victories and defeats, his fears and dreams. And he had listened to her fears, her plans for the future, her song lyrics, her dreams.

And now—

Why did this have to happen? Why, when everything in her life was so wonderful, did tragedy have to visit? Why did this collision of dream and reality always have to occur?—as if no good fortune was possible without a balancing amount of evil. What sort of god would have set such a mechanism in motion?

Face to face with that portion of the universe revealed by the starlight, Minmei began to cry. Later she would bang her fists against the rail of the balcony and curse those stars, then sink back against the wooden slats of the bench and surrender to her sorrow. And ultimately she would retrieve from her handbag a penlight she carried there, and, aiming it toward the ship's bay, she would click it on and off, again and again, a light signal into "forever" of her undying affection for him.

CHAPTER
FIFTEEN

*Spirit does not willingly abdicate its throne. The Big
Bang was Spirit's first rebellion against form—its imprison-
ment in matter. Subsequently it fought humankind's accep-
tance of fire; it battled against steam; it contested electricity
and nuclear power; it raged against Protoculture . . . War is
Spirit's attempt to attain freedom from matter, its effort to
remain autonomous. Wars are waged to prevent matter from
becoming too comfortable or complacent. For it is Spirit's
divine purpose to someday abandon its vehicle and tran-
scend, to reunite with the Godhead and suck the universe
back into itself.*

Reverend Houston, from the foreword to Jan Morris's
Solar Seeds, Galactic Guardians

Protoculture is technology's royal jelly.

Dr. Emil Lang

UNKNOWN TO BREETAI OR HIS CREW, THERE WAS A
stowaway aboard the Zentraedi flagship—a Micronian
Veritech ace named Max Sterling.

Sucked into space through the hole in the hull created
by Rick Hunter's self-destructed Battloid, Max had un-
knowingly duplicated the walk Breetai had undertaken
along the outer surface of the ship sometime earlier.
Breetai, however, was familiar with the manual air lock
mechanisms, so he merely had to let himself in; Max had
to discover a way in. Fortunately he had stumbled upon

an unclosed breach in the hull—the fried bristle sensors surrounding the hole gave evidence of a previous explosion—flown himself into an empty bay, and, returned to Battloid mode, made his way into the ship through an unlocked hatchway. His gatling cannon had been left in the hold, his lasers were burned out, and he had scarcely half a dozen rockets left. Max was operating on willpower, driven by the hope of rescuing his friends.

The interior of the flagship was a labyrinth of corridors and serviceways, some well lighted and maintained, others dark, damp, and in varying states of disrepair. But luckily, all of them had been deserted.

Until now.

Max was at the intersection of two corridors—curved ceilings, large overhead light banks—peering around the corner when he saw the alien enter. A private, Max guessed: standard-issue drab highrise-collared uniform, a round cap with an insignia. He moved the Battloid back a step and scanned the area. A short distance down the corridor behind him was what appeared to be a utility closet with a curved-top hatch. He made his way to this as quickly and quietly as he could manage, threw the bolt, and secreted the mecha inside. Shut off from the corridor, Max had no way of knowing which route the Zentraedi had taken, so the look of surprise on the alien's face upon discovering a Battloid in the utility closet was no greater than the startled look on Max's own.

For what seemed like an eternity they both stood there marveling at each other, until Max's training brought a decisive end to it. He executed a sidekick with the Battloid's right foot that caught the Zentraedi's midsection, instantly doubling him over. Gathering up the unconscious private in the Battloid's right arm, Max stretched out the left, grabbed the door bolt, and slammed the hatch shut.

He was puzzling over what to do with the guy, when all at once the cockpit indicators began crying out for attention. He checked the readouts but still couldn't make sense of anything: All systems were functioning, and there didn't seem to be any immediate threats to the mecha, environmentally or otherwise. So what was going on?

Then Max glanced at the astrogation displays. The temporal sensors were spinning wildly—the flagship was *folding*!

Max watched as hours and days began to accrue on the gauge. He slumped into his seat and waited . . .

The emergency spacefold which had catapulted the SDF-1 and Macross City clear across the solar system had been Lisa's first; and, as such, there hadn't been time to . . . well, *look around*. It had also been a relatively short jump through space and therefore a brief one through time. But for this, her second trip through the continuum, the temporal indicator built into her suit registered the equivalent of fourteen Earth-days. Wherever the Zentraedi were going, it was a long way from home.

Lisa had plenty of time to look around.

It was nothing like she had expected, nothing, in fact, like she had been *trained* to expect. The stars did not so much disappear as come and go. She couldn't be certain, however, that it was the *same* stars that were rematerializing each time. The heavens seemed altered with each fade, as though someone had snipped frames from a strip of film, editing out the transitions from event to event. The energy umbrella that kept her and the others confined to the grid prevented her from observing flux details in the laboratory, but when she looked at Rick or Ben, she noticed a slight shimmering effect that blurred the boundaries of objects; occasionally, this effect intensified so that there was a sense of double focus to everything: the form of the past, the form of the future, distinct, discrete, unable to unite.

In real time, one Earth-day elapsed; and as the flagship began to decelerate from hyperspace, the past twenty-four hours took on a dreamlike quality. Had she slept through most of it, dreamed a good part of it? Or was this some new condition of consciousness yet to be named?

Lisa, Rick, and Ben stood at the edge of their small world, watching the stars assume lasting form once again. These were alien configurations to their eyes: brilliant constellations of suns, dwarfs and giants, three planets or moons of some unknown system, all against the backdrop of a gauzy multihued nebulosity. And something else—something their unadjusted vision labeled an asteroid field, so numerous were the dark objects in that corner of space.

"What are those things?" asked Ben.

"Space debris," Rick suggested. "We might be near their home base."

Lisa squinted; then her eyes opened wide in amazement.

Not asteroids, not space debris, but ships: amorphous ships as far as the eye could see, ships bristling with guns, too numerous to count, too numerous to catalogue —scouts, recons, destroyers, cruisers, battle wagons, flagships. Thousands of ships, *millions* of them!

"The enemy fleet!"

It was too much to take in, but Lisa used the microvideo recorder the aliens had overlooked to capture what she could.

More than a year would pass before they learned the exact count; a day of reckoning . . .

The flagship was now closing on a dazzling cluster of lights, a kind of force field that housed an immeasurable asymmetrical fortress their senses refused to comprehend.

But they soon had other issues to confront. Without warning, the energy umbrella had been deactivated and the circumstances of their world redefined. They had wondered how their captors had been able to provide them with food and drink served on human-size plates, with cups and utensils in proper proportion. But there would be no such comfort for them from this moment on.

Two giants now stood on either side of the grid, which turned out to be some sort of specimen table. Could anything have prepared them for the assault of sensations that followed—the deafening basso rumble of the giants' voices, the sonorous roar of their mecha and machines, the intensity of the corridor lights, the overpowering smells of hyperoxygenated air, stale breath, sweat, and decay?

They were transferred to a second platform—a hover-table directed through the corridors by their jailers—and ultimately to a gleaming conference table as large as a football field. There were banks of overhead lights and several chairs positioned around the table. Lisa noticed that amplifiers had been strategically positioned here and there—*the better to hear you with, my dear*! And one by one their interrogators entered the room and sat down.

The first to arrive was a male scarcely half the size of those Zentraedi they'd seen. A slightly hunched back was evident beneath his blue cowl; swollen joints and outsize hands and feet suggested some sort of birth defect. He had an inverted bowl of henna hair thick as straw concealing a deformed cranium, uneven bangs bisecting a high forehead above a drawn face, and bulging, seemingly lidless eyes with pinpoint pupils. He was carrying notebooks, which he placed on the table next to a light-board device; this he activated as he sat down, bending forward to regard his three prisoners analytically.

Next to enter the chamber was the immense soldier Rick had battled in the hold; there was no forgetting that faceplate, no forgetting that malicious grin. Trailing behind him were three more males of differing heights, wearing identical red uniforms, not one of them as short as the disabled Zentraedi or as tall as their commander. They took seats at the far end of the table.

Lisa was wondering who or what was going to fill the empty seat between the commander and his adviser; when the answer to her whispered question arrived, she was at once sorry she had asked.

"How many sizes do these guys come in?" said Ben in amazement.

The grand inquisitor stood well over eighty feet tall and wore a solemn gray robe with a high upturned collar that all but enclosed his massive, hairless head. The heavy brow ridge, pockmarked sullen face, and wide mouth gave him a fearful aspect, and when he spoke there was no mistaking his meaning.

"I am Dolza," he began. "Commander-in-Chief of the Zentraedi. You will submit to my interrogation. Should you choose not to, you will die. Do you understand me?"

Rick, Ben, and Lisa looked at one another, realizing suddenly that they had failed to elect a spokesperson—for the simple reason that they hadn't expected an actual session with the enemy. The fact that they would be able to communicate with the Zentraedi gave them new hope.

Lisa secretly activated the audio receiver of the microrecorder, while Rick stepped forward to speak for his group.

"We understand you. What do you want from us?"

Dolza turned to the dwarf. "Congratulations, Exedore, you have done well in teaching me their primitive language."

Exedore inclined his head slightly.

"Why do you continue to resist us, Micronians?" Dolza gestured to the male on his right. "Surely Breetai has already demonstrated our superiority."

Rick pointed his finger at the one called Breetai. "You launched the attack on *us*! We've only been trying to defend ourselves for the past year—"

"Immaterial," Breetai interrupted. "Return to us what is rightfully ours—Zor's ship."

"'Zor's ship'? If you mean the SDF-1, that's our property. It crashed on our planet, and we rebuilt it. You—"

Dolza cut Rick off. "It is as I feared," he said to Exedore.

"Tell us what you know of Protoculture. You—the fat one."

Ben gestured to himself questioningly. "Me? Forget it, high rise. I don't know anything about it."

"Tell us what you know of Protoculture!" Dolza demanded.

"You deny that you've developed a new weapons system utilizing Protoculture?" Exedore wanted to know.

Rick turned to his companions and shrugged. The questions kept up, increasing in volume, until Lisa decided she'd had enough. She stepped forward boldly and held up her hand.

"That's enough! I will no longer submit my men to your questioning!"

Dolza raised what he had of eyebrows. "So the female is in charge here." He sat back in his chair, steepling his fingers as he did so. "You underestimate the seriousness of your predicament, Micronian."

And with a wave of his hand the room was transformed.

Lisa, Rick, and Ben were suddenly in deep . . . *space*! At least it appeared that way: Here were the stars, planets, and tens of thousands of ships they had seen upon defold into Zentraedi territory. And yet they had not moved from the table, and Dolza's voice could still be heard narrating the phenomenal events occurring in that unreal space.

Photon charges were beginning to build up in several of the fleet ships; they were taking aim at a planet not unlike Earth in appearance . . .

"We are in possession of sufficient power to destroy your world in the blink of an eye," Dolza was saying. "And if you need proof of that, behold . . ."

As lethal rays from the battle wagons and cruisers converged on the living surface of the planet, a glow of death began to spread and encompass it; and when that fatal light faded, a lifeless, cratered sphere was all that remained.

Lisa hung her head; the Zentraedi had just destroyed a planet merely to make a point. Is this what they had planned for Earth? But then, why were they holding back? What had Exedore said about "a new weapons system utilizing *Protoculture*"? She made up her mind to try a bluff.

"You don't have enough power to destroy the SDF-1, Dolza."

"Impertinence!" their interrogator yelled.

Ignoring Rick's plea for caution, she continued: "The SDF-1 has powers you've never dreamed of."

Dolza brought his fists down on the table, throwing the Terrans off their feet. He then reached out and grabbed Lisa in his right hand. He brought her close to his face, warning Rick and Ben to stay put.

"Now, my feisty female, I want to know by what

process you become Micronians." He tightened his grip around Lisa, demanding an immediate answer.

"Stop squeezing her!" said Rick. "We're born this way. We're born . . . *Micronian*!"

"Born from *what* is the question," said Exedore.

"Huh? Well . . . from our mothers. What else?"

"What is this thing you call 'mother'?" one of the Zentraedi behind Rick asked.

Ben swung around to face the red-uniformed trio.

"Mother. You know, like the parent that's female." Ben turned to Rick, twirling his forefinger against his temple.

Exedore was startled. "You mean that you are actually *born* from the females of your kind?"

Breetai was incredulous.

"Hey," Ben continued. "It happens, you know. You put a man and a woman together and . . . well, it just happens." He laughed. "It's love."

Breetai looked over at Dolza, then fixed his gaze on Ben. "'Love,' yes, I have heard that word mentioned in some of your transmissions. But what is it? How do you express it?"

"Oh, brother," Ben said under his breath. "You field this one, Commander."

Rick shot him a look and chuckled, in spite of himself, in spite of the gravity of the situation. "It can start with a kiss, I guess."

Dolza wasn't buying it: If Micronians could be produced by kissing, then he wanted living proof of it. He ordered Rick and Ben to demonstrate.

"Demonstrate this kissing or I will crush all of you!"

Rick was stammering an explanation of the facts, when he heard Lisa agree to volunteer. Released from Dolza's grip, she staggered weakly over to Rick, leaning against him as though regaining her strength and taking advantage of their proximity to explain her plan: She wanted Rick to kiss her...so she could record the aliens' reaction on her microcamera.

Rick stepped away from her. "Do it with Ben, Commander."

She turned and looked over at the corporal briefly. "Listen, Rick, I'd rather do it with you, all right?"

"You'll have to make it a command, sir."

"Proceed at once!" said Dolza.

Lisa held Rick's gaze, softening his anger somewhat by the hurt look he thought he saw in her eyes.

"I'm giving you a direct order, Lieutenant Hunter: Kiss me."

Rick made a silent appeal for Minmei's forgiveness and stepped into Lisa's arms. They kissed each other full on the mouth, and for several seconds the two of them were far away from it all. It was, however, difficult to sustain that romantic mood while six giants were making sick sounds behind their backs. They broke their embrace and stepped apart.

"What is happening to us?" said Dolza. "This results from Protoculture?"

"It is their weapons system at work," said Exedore.

Dolza was on his feet, glaring at the Terrans. "Take them out of here at once! Get these Mirconians out of my sight!"

Rick turned to Lisa as the three of them were being herded onto the hover-table once again. "Are we *that* bad at it?"

She looked at him and said, "I guess we are."

CHAPTER
SIXTEEN

> *"Ya gotta picture it, gang: I mean, here's Rick, Lisa, and Ben, surrounded by these six giants, Hunter and Hayes step into each other's arms, liplock, and these big, bad hombres begin to freak! I mean . . . [laughs shortly], 'magine if Lisa's microcamera had been set up to show X-rated movies? The war woulda been over on the spot!"*
>
> Unnamed VT pilot, as quoted by Rick Hunter

> *"What's love got to do with it?"*
>
> Late twentieth-century song lyric

DOLZA AND HIS ADVISORY GROUP REMAINED IN the interrogation room after the Mirconian prisoners had been taken away. The Zentraedi commander in chief was disturbed by the reactions he had experienced when the female and male had kissed each other. Breetai stated that he had felt weakened after witnessing a verbal argument between these same two Micronians; and apparently, similar feelings had plagued the three operatives of the surveillance team that had been dispatched to monitor transmissions from Zor's ship. Now, as Dolza listened to the recon team's report, he asked himself whether Exedore's suspicions about the Micronian use of Protoculture might not be justified, after all. Perhaps he should have killed Zor when he had had the chance, or simply destroyed the dimensional fortress, instead of seeing in it a road to freedom for himself and the rest of his warrior race.

"...and Konda here had the same reaction when he saw the unclothed female," Rico, the commander of the team, was saying.

"It's true, sir," Konda affirmed. "Although I didn't agree at the time."

"This could only be done with Protoculture," said Dolza. He folded his arms and addressed the group. "What I'm about to tell you must never leave this room. Is that understood?"

Breetai and Exedore nodded their assent. In unison, Rico, Konda, and Bron said, "Yes, sir!"

"Protoculture, as Breetai and Exedore are aware, is the essence of Robotechnology developed by our ancestors. Yes, *ancestors*," he emphasized for the sake of the recon team. "In the beginning, members of the Zentraedi race were the same size as these Micronians. And at one time we, too, lived together, male and female, in something that was called a 'society.' But through the use of Protoculture we were able to evolve to our present size, strength, and superiority. However, a series of events that must even now be kept secret from you led to a loss of our understanding of Protoculture."

Dolza put his open hands on the table and leaned forward.

"I have every reason to believe that those lost secrets are to be found aboard Zor's ship." He allowed this to sink in for a moment. "This is why the Micronians present such a potential threat. And this is precisely why we must take that ship back undamaged."

"We have not been able to determine to what extent the Micronians have applied their understanding of Protoculture," Breetai added. "But it is obvious to me that they know enough to effect repairs on Robotech equipment and perhaps enough to be experimenting with a new weapons system."

"Sir," said Rico. "We have demonstrated our power to them. Why not hold their planet hostage for the return of the ship?"

It was a generally unheard of notion, but Dolza was willing to entertain it. He stroked his chin and turned to Exedore.

"You have made a thorough study of this race. You appear to have an understanding of their language and culture. Would such a threat be effective?"

Exedore weighed his words carefully. "Sir, it is not the Zentraedi way to speak of past defeats, but may I be permitted to remind this table that these Micronians have already demonstrated an uncommon determination to survive. In response to our initial attacks on their homeworld, the commander of the ship, with no regard for the lives of tens of thousands of his fellow creatures, executed an intraatmospheric spacefold to escape us. This same commander detonated a reflex furnace on the fourth planet in their system, endangering the ship and the lives of all aboard rather than surrender to Commander Khyron's mechanized division. Even though crippled in space and without radar, they simply ignored our most recent demands for surrender . . . In response then to your query, my lord: No, I do not think that such a plan would work."

"We cannot risk losing those secrets," said Dolza. "We must infiltrate the ship and determine what the Micronians know about Protoculture."

Breetai, who knew Zor's ship inside and out, had a plan he began to relate to Dolza. Rico, Konda, and Bron, meanwhile, hatched a plan of their own: They made a joint decision to volunteer to go through the cellular transformation process which enabled a Zentraedi to assume Micronian dimensions.

Dolza and Breetai would find the trio's proposal acceptable, and later, even commendable. And fortunately for Rico and the others, they were never called upon to give reasons for their sudden dedication to the cause. Because if the truth were known, all this talk about Robotechnology and Protoculture was way beyond them. They were simply anxious to have another look at those partially clothed Mirconian females and experience again those curious feelings that were the result.

In a holding cell elsewhere on Breetai's ship, Lisa, Rick, and Ben, sitting in a patch of corridor light which poured through cellular windows in the chamber's double doors, were comparing their own reactions to the Zentraedi interrogation. It was a little like being locked in an empty airliner hangar, but at least there were no giants on the scene.

"It was the weirdest thing I've seen in a while," Ben was saying. "You two kiss, and the big guys go nuts. I don't get it."

"They have enough power to atomize the Earth, but simple contact is too much for them to handle," said Rick.

Lisa was deep in thought.

"And what about this 'Protoculture' business? What do you think, Commander?"

Lisa looked at Ben. "Do you realize that we haven't seen any female Zentraedi? No children, no civilians, not even any techs or maintenance crews. Only soldiers."

"We haven't exactly been given the grand tour," Rick reminded her.

"I realize that, Lieutenant. But it could be that there *are* no females of their kind."

"No, that can't be. They know you're female. They had some kind of knowledge about mothers and birth."

"Lieutenant, we gotta get outta here," Ben said, looking around.

"I know. I've been giving it some thought. We might be able to use our new weapon on them."

"What new weapon? What are you talking about?"

Rick smacked his lips. "The kiss. Don't you get it? We wait till the guard comes with our food, we confuse him with our, uh, weapon, and we make a break for it."

Ben was already on his feet. "Great! Any place'll be better than this."

Lisa looked at the two of them. "Are you joking? You mean that every time a Zentraedi shows his face we're going to put on a show for him? Forget it, Lieutenant. I've heard some lines in my day, but that one beats them all."

Rick's mouth dropped open. "Just hold it a minute, *Commander*. Whose idea was it in the first place? Besides, if you think I'm doing this because I want to, you've got another—"

"That'll be enough, mister! I only kissed you to get their reaction on tape." She patted the camera. "We've got it now; we don't need to do another take."

Ben stepped forward, "Hey, listen, I'm perfectly willing to volunteer to be your partner, Commander Hayes."

"At ease, Corporal," Lisa told him.

She turned her back on the two of them, angry but

wondering: Was there anything about strategic osculation in the officers' manual?

Help was on the way.

In what was certainly the most complicated set of mecha-motions executed to date, Max Sterling had managed to clothe his Battloid in the uniform he had taken from the Zentraedi private. That he had succeeded so completely in wedding his mind to the mecha controls was justification enough for the many articles later devoted to the feat, but the fact that he had accomplished this within the confines of the utility closet was what ultimately led to his legendary status as a VT hero.

Making certain the Zentraedi was neatly tied up and stowed away, Max checked the corridor, eased out of the closet, and began to follow his instincts. The Zentraedi uniform was well suited to the Battloid's purpose, the high-collared jacket especially so. And even with the round cap pulled low, the cockpit wide-angle and long-range cameras and scanners had enough clearance for operation.

Not ten paces down the hallway, Max encountered one of the massively built, armored shock troopers, who luckily paid him little notice. Now having passed the test, he began to move with increased confidence, and not long after he spotted two of the enemy guiding a hover-table through the ship. Max upped the magnification on his cameras, locked in on the table, and found Lisa, Ben, and Rick, looking none the worse for wear but in no condition to do battle with their giant captors.

Max trailed the guards at a discreet distance and watched as Lieutenant Hunter and the others were deposited in some sort of double-doored holding cell. A single sentry was posted outside.

Max was not inclined to wait much longer; besides, the sentry was already betraying his boredom with yawns and general inattentiveness. Max primed the Battloid for action and moved in.

When Lisa heard the commotion in the corridor outside the cell, she had a change in heart: Maybe Hunter's plan would work. There wasn't much to lose at this point, so she convinced herself that kissing him was just part of the mission. She told him so, and the two of them readied their "secret weapon" while Ben waited by the door.

Though Max's reaction to throwing open the cell door and finding his commanders locked in a loving embrace was more pure surprise than anything else, his temporary paralysis convinced the prisoners that they had made the right move. The three were ready to bolt for the corridor when Max opened the external com net and called out to them.

"It's me—Max!"

They stopped in midstride and stared up at him.

"M-Max?" Rick said tentatively.

"Yeah, I'm in here all right."

"God, Max, we thought you were dead," said Lisa.

"Yeah, well, long story."

Ben wanted to know where the uniform had come from.

"Later. We better get a move on." He lowered the Battloid's gloved left hand. Rick and Lisa climbed in, and Max raised it up, leaving Ben on the floor.

"Hey, man!"

"Hang on, Ben, I want you in the other hand."

Ben climbed into the lowered right. Now Max brought both the Battloid's hands level with the uniform's breast pockets. Lisa and Rick grabbed hold of the

insignia-pocket and pulled themselves in; Ben did like-
wise on the other side of the jacket.

"I don't want you to interrupt the lovebirds, Ben."

"Now wait a minute, Corporal," Lisa protested. "We
only did that to escape."

"Kissing each other to escape, huh? I understand."

"Listen up, Max—"

"Save it, Lieutenant. You've got my word that I won't
spread this around Macross City. Although I must say
you had me fooled. I thought you preferred younger
women."

"Max!"

"Get yourselves down in there. We're moving out."

Rick held in his anger and slid down into the pocket
alongside Lisa. The Battloid parted the double hatches
of the holding cell and began to take long, stiff strides
down the corridor.

It wasn't long before they heard Max utter a sound of
alert. A Zentraedi soldier, armored and armed with a hip
blaster, was approaching them. Soldier and disguised
Battloid passed each other seemingly without incident,
and inside the pocket Rick and Lisa breathed a prema-
ture sigh of relief.

But the soldier had stopped and was calling for Max
to halt.

Max was in no position to defend himself or his pas-
sengers; launching his few remaining rockets would have
fried Rick and Lisa. So he took the only course available: He ran—straight into two more shock troopers
who were coming down the corridor. Max tackled one of
them, lifting him and swinging him into the other as he
continued on his way, but by now the first soldier was
chasing him and opening fire. He was quickly joined by
his comrades.

The Battloid sustained blasterbolt after blasterbolt to the back as it flew through the ship, pieces of burned and tattered cloth flying in its wake. At Rick's urging, Max reconfigured the VT to Guardian mode, ripping open the uniform jacket as he hit the aft thrusters. In that hail of lethal fire, the Guardian looked like some sort of caped bird of prey fighting its way to freedom.

Corridor length, however, was suddenly in short supply, and Max knew the VT wouldn't be able to pull off a ninety-degree turn in such limited space. Set in the bulkhead at the top of the corridor T, however, was a control panel which could probably be pierced without undue damage to the fighter. Max opted for it and pulled the thruster lever home.

The bulkhead surrendered too easily, and by the time Max realized that the VT had broken through a large circular viewing screen in a control room, the Guardian was way beyond it, tearing through a series of projec-beam astrogational charts free-floating in an immense central chamber of the ship. An open rectangular port at the far end of the room delivered them into another serviceway, at the end of which was a sealed elevator. They were still taking rear fire when the elevator doors parted. A surprised Zentraedi soldier saw them coming and leaped out into the corridor, narrowly escaping impalement on the radome of the VT.

Once inside the cubicle, Max blew the canopy and clambered out onto the arm of the craft, clutching his laser rifle.

"The circuits are fried! This thing's gonna blow!"

Rick left the pocket and catwalked the extended arm of the Guardian to the elevator closure lever. He jumped up and grabbed hold of it, riding it down as the doors closed. The fighter was temporarily sealed off from enemy fire, and the elevator began to descend.

One, two, three, four, five levels and they were still going down, the Guardian giving off predestruct noises and smoke now, Max and the others offering up silent prayers for the doors to open.

At level six the elevator stopped. The doors parted, and the four defenders were off and running. But out of nowhere a Zentraedi shock trooper made an airborne grab for them, landing facedown and miraculously empty-handed in front of the elevator. The soldier got to his feet, his quarry long gone, and stared at the smoldering uniformed thing inside.

He had perhaps a second to contemplate its crouched birdlike form before the ensuing explosion blew him away.

If the soldier's last grasp failed to capture the four, it had at least succeeded in dividing them.

Rick and Lisa ran for quite a while before realizing that Ben and Max were no longer with them. They searched for a while, but the explosion of the VT had drawn more Zentraedi to the scene, and it seemed a wiser move to push on.

They entered an area where several corridors converged. It was a vast, domed chamber crowded with generators, computer terminals, conduits, and ductwork. There was an overpowering smell to the place, as alien as anything their senses had yet encountered, and a sonic roar that reminded them of pressure-cooker sounds, amplified and low-frequency-enhanced. They secreted themselves behind a long console covered with switches and control knobs. Then, cautiously, they peered over the top.

What they saw was a cluster of thirty-meter-high vessels, like medicinal capsules stood on end, transparent and filled with a purple viscous, churning fluid. In at least six of these vessels were half-formed, featureless Zentraedi. Rick was totally bewildered and vaguely upset by the sight, but Lisa's sharp intake of breath told him that she recognized something here.

"So *that's* why so many of the Zentraedi soldiers look alike—they're all clones!"

Lisa risked a better view: Now she could see a second cluster of human-size capsules positioned in front of the larger ones, also churning, also containing some half-formed shape. It took her a moment to make sense of this, and when she turned to Rick with an explanation, she scarcely believed her own words: The Zentraedi were reducing their soldiers to human size.

Rick looked at her like she was crazy, and she didn't blame him. But there it was, happening right before their eyes, and no other explanation was forthcoming.

They pulled back as more soldiers entered the chamber searching for them and resumed their conversation some distance away in a dimly lit weapons room.

"You remember how Dolza kept asking us how we became Micronians?"

"Yeah, so?"

"They're wondering if we have similar clone chambers and reduction devices. That's why they can't understand any closeness between the sexes, because, well, love and sex wouldn't be necessary in a society of clones."

"Incredible."

"You're not kidding, incredible. And it wouldn't surprise me to learn that Zentraedi and humans are genetically related. In the beginning they were probably the same size as us!"

"So what are they, human giants or giant humans?"

She looked at him blankly. "I guess it's too early to say. Maybe after we analyze the videos we'll know. But right now, I'd say they can go either way. They've found some way of rearranging their molecular structure—big for hostile environments, small for..." Lisa shrugged.

"Yeah," said Rick. "Small for what? Why are they *reducing* some of their troops? And how are they doing it?"

"Protoculture," Lisa said evenly.

The word had scarcely left her lips when Rick heard the growl. Suddenly a giant hand reached into the room and took hold of Lisa. She screamed. Rick yelled and gave chase, mindless of the consequences.

The giant had straightened from his crouch by the time Rick hit the corridor; he was holding Lisa near his face, growling at her. As Rick ran into view, the Zentraedi soldier simply extended his foot—not a kick, really, but more than enough to lift Rick off the floor and send him careening into a rack of upright laser rifles. Why every bone in his body wasn't broken, he had no idea (*adrenaline*, he'd tell himself later), but at the moment all he knew was that he was buried under the weapons, stunned and crushed but alive and angrier than ever.

Rick allowed the fear and anger to get hold of him; he positioned himself on one knee and heaved one of the rifles over his shoulder like a bazooka—a five-meter-long bazooka. Putting all his meager weight to the trigger, he managed to yank off three rapid blasts. The Zentraedi caught all of them—one through the fish eye face-shield and two through the pectoral armor—and went down like an oak. Rick dropped the weapon and rushed in to find Lisa still in the soldier's hand, crying.

He stopped in his tracks, then moved in slowly, afraid to touch or move her.

"Jeez, Lisa...how bad are you hurt?"

"I dropped the camera, I—I...it shattered."

"Forget the camera! You mean you're not hurt?"

"No, I don't think so. But the mission..."

"Unbelievable," Rick muttered as he helped her from the slack hand. "Sometimes women just don't make any sense, even when they're officers."

It wasn't in any way meant to bring her around, but it surely did: She threw him off and ran a hand over her wet eyes. "Don't start with me, Hunter."

Rick felt the footsteps coming. He grabbed her hand, and the chase was on again. *This has got to be the way mice feel*, he told himself while they were running.

The Zentraedi soldiers were right on top of them, forcing them into left and right turns indiscriminately. Ultimately they found themselves in a dark and deteriorated corridor, with stress fissures in the walls and great gaping holes in the floor. Explosive bolts of energy threw light and short-lived shadows all around them as they ran. And suddenly the world dropped out from under them, light and sound beginning to fade as they plunged toward emptiness together...

CHAPTER
SEVENTEEN

*The list of players was still incomplete when Miriya took
to the stage; but was there ever a harder act to follow?*

The Collected Journals of Admiral Rick Hunter

THE BEST THEY COULD DO WAS CLEAN UP THE MESS.

Breetai looked on as two lower-echelon soldiers
carted fragments of the broken viewscreen from the
bridge. The front shield of the observation bubble was
also in ruin. Much as Breetai's career.

Dolza, Breetai, and Exedore had been on the bridge
when the Micronians' mecha had punched through the
wall. Only seconds before, they had been informed of
the prisoners' escape, and Breetai was promising their
speedy recapture. Then, suddenly, the transformed Battloid had exploded into their midst and soared belliger-

ently out across the astrogation hold. Breetai had glimpsed the look on Dolza's face then, and now that look was being leveled against him.

"So, Breetai, have the Micronians been recaptured?"

"I'm sorry to report that they haven't. Their size presents difficulties."

The Zentraedi commander-in-chief cocked his head to one side. "Indeed. And further difficulties are the last thing we need at the moment. Do you understand?"

"M'lord."

"The responsibility was yours, and this failure will have to be entered into the record." Dolza turned his back to Breetai. "I am relieving you of active duty for the time being, Commander."

He turned around and motioned to the shattered observation bubble. "You can hardly continue to operate in this . . . *condition*, in any case."

It was even worse than Breetai had expected. But he thought there might still be a way out. Exedore stepped forward to speak for him.

"But sir, the infiltration—who will assume responsibility for the operation?"

Dolza considered this. "Breetai's knowledge of Zor's ship has been an invaluable aid to us in this matter. It will be duly noted. However, Azonia will now be in charge of our three agents."

"Azonia?!" Breetai and Exedore exclaimed.

"But Azonia isn't briefed—"

Dolza held up his hand to silence Exedore. "Commander Azonia is a loyal subject who has never failed me. Once more, I am assigning our finest pilot to her charge."

Just then two soldiers requested entry and conveyed the hover-table onto the bridge. Grouped together on the tabletop and clothed in the only suitable garments available—sleeveless sackcloths cinched at the waist by rough cords—were the three now "micronized" operatives, Rico, Konda, and Bron.

Dolza looked down on them soberly.

"You understand the gravity of your mission?"

"Sir!" three small voices shouted in unison.

"Miriya will oversee your insertion into the dimensional fortress."

The agents exchanged looks and expressions of excitement.

"Succeed and you will each have a cruiser to command upon your return."

Three arms were raised in salute: "For the glory of the Zentraedi!"

Dolza returned the salute and turned to Breetai as the hover-table was taken from the bridge.

"This time we will not fail."

Ben remembered having hurdled the giant alien's spread fingers, but Max assured him that he'd done nothing of the sort. They'd both taken a dive off to one side of the corridor when the Zentraedi pounced and found cover behind an open hatch just as the VT exploded. They saw Rick and the Commander make their escape, but neither Max nor Ben was able to pick up the trail. While enemy soldiers poured into the area, the two corporals had moved swiftly through a serviceway that ran parallel to the ship's central corridor. They had made good progress for several hours, until Max had inadvertently tripped a scanner alarm reset to detect movement along the floor of the passageway.

They had three shock troopers on their tail now and a deadly flock of projectiles overhead. The soldiers were herding them toward a waiting elevator, hoping to corner them inside. But perhaps the enemy hadn't identified the weapon one of the Micronians carried, or perhaps they hadn't even seen it? In any case, no sooner did the two enter the car than Max swung himself about face, trained his laser rifle on the elevator controls, and fired. The intense beam soldered the proper circuits; the doors slid closed, and the car began to descend . . .

In that liquid dream, Minmei was leaving him and Rick was calling out to her, over and over again . . .

Then Lisa's face floated into focus, and the dream faded. She helped him sit up and asked if he was all right.

He began to take stock of himself and these new dark and wet surroundings. They were in an area of huge pipes, containment chambers, baffles, valves, and regulating devices, seated near the edge of a system of channels and reservoirs that stretched out into the darkness. Shafts of light filtered down from far above them, and the thick air was filled with the sounds of mechanized pumps and filtration units, running water, and the clank and hiss of fluid control conduits.

They were both soaked to the skin; Lisa's uncoiled long brown hair hung in wet waves halfway down her back.

She said, "We must be in the water-recycling chamber. It's in terrible disrepair." She laughed at her words. "Great time to be judgmental, huh? This pool saved our lives. We must have fallen a hundred feet."

With effort, Rick got to his feet. "Maybe the water broke our fall, but something else saved me from drowning."

Lisa averted his gaze. "I wasn't about to have you die on me, Hunter." Then she looked directly at him. "Let's just call it even."

Rick's vision was adapting itself to the dark; he began to take notice of the refuse and debris all around them.

Nearby there were hatchways and elevator platforms, and somewhere in the distance, faint light.

"They do let things get run-down, don't they?"

"I've been thinking about it, Lieutenant. Even with all their technical knowledge, maybe they only know how to *use* the equipment but not how to repair it. No techs, no maintenance personnel. Just soldier clones, every last one of them."

"All this destructive power...I wonder how many worlds they've ended, how many lives they've taken. It's sickening to think about: an entire civilization dedicated to war."

"I guess I should feel right at home."

"What d' ya mean?"

"My father had a favorite saying: 'Only where there is battle being waged is there life being lived.'" She sighed. "My family has been connected with the military for the past century...The only life I've ever known is the Defense Forces. 'The mission,' that's all I can think about." She gestured. "You heard me up there."

"Yeah, but that's why you're an officer. You're a leader. Head of the class and all that."

Lisa's eyebrows knitted. "How did you find that out?"

"It's common knowledge." Rick laughed. "Some of the VT pilots call you Supergirl."

"Wonderful..." She looked hard at Rick. "You know, I don't mean to intimidate anyone. It's just that..." A sly smile replaced her grim expression. "Forget it. But I'll bet Miss Macross isn't a bit intimidating, is she?"

Rick was taken off guard. "Minmei? What makes you think—"

"You were calling her name: 'Minmei! Minmei!'" Lisa playfully mocked him.

"All right, all right. What of it?"

"You tell me."

"Nothing to tell. We're friends, that's all. You know how it is. She's a celebrity. Public property. We don't have time for each other anymore."

"A major talent, I'm sure."

Rick gave her a look that signaled she'd gone too far.

"Listen, Lieutenant, I'm only kidding. At least you *have* someone to return to. All I have is another mission to look forward to."

"There's no one in your life?"

"Just call me Miss SDF-1."

"That's just a matter of time. You're a beautiful woman. Most guys would give..."

"Yeah?"

"What I mean is, you're a brilliant officer, and..."

Lisa didn't say anything for a minute; then she cleared her throat and stood up. "Well, I'm not going to meet anyone sitting around here, am I?"

She took hold of Rick's hand. "Let's get out of here, Lieutenant."

They walked toward the light.

Engine rooms, storage rooms, empty holds, a second recycling plant, more storage areas—all in the same shabby, unwashed, and unmaintained state. But something had changed: The air had begun to lose that over-poweringly dank smell and thickness. A slight breeze played through Lisa's long hair.

They moved toward the source of the wind.

At the far end of a supply room filled with Battlepods and ordnance of every conceivable type, they found their exit: a rectangular port in the hull of the ship. They ran toward this, the wind no longer gentle but chilled and full of sound, and stopped short of the edge, awestruck.

So wrapped up in finding a way out, they had forgotten that they were actually onboard a ship within a ship!

If you could call it a ship.

Beyond the portal was a sight their senses were unprepared for: hundreds of Zentraedi ships anchored weightless in the seemingly sky-blue docking chamber of the command center. Overcome by a sudden wave of vertigo, Lisa took a step back. Was it possible? Dolza's ship would have to be the best kept secret in the universe—a thousand miles long—to accommodate all these vessels! Her mind wrestled with it, her thoughts spinning out of control.

Rick had taken hold of her arm. "Someone's coming!" he told her.

They concealed themselves behind some crates near the portal. Rick tuned in to the sounds he had heard and realized at once that no Zentraedi was capable of making so little noise. It had to be . . .

"Ben! Max!" Lisa yelled.

The four of them reunited in a group embrace, and capsule summaries of their respective adventures and ordeals were rapidly exchanged. Max complimented Lisa on how lovely she looked with her hair down, and she congratulated him on having been able to hang on to his "thinking cap" all this time. Ben was in his usual good humor.

"So what's next on the agenda, friends?"

The intrusion of reality cooled their warm reunion somewhat; what was next, indeed? From the edge of the portal they could see a cruiser taking on supplies through a transfer tube at a neighboring port in the flagship.

"We could get aboard easy enough," said Max, "but where do you think she's bound?"

"Does it matter?" Ben asked. "Let's go."

"Hold on a minute, Ben," said Lisa. "We were

brought here on this ship. I think we'd stand a better chance of getting back to the SDF-1 by remaining aboard."

Max didn't like the idea. "Not if the Zentraedi capture us. We've seen too much by now. They won't take any chances with us."

"He's right," Rick agreed. "You're in charge, Lisa, but I vote for the cruiser."

Lisa crossed her arms, then relaxed and smiled at them.

"All right, let's do it."

They set off at once.

Finding their way to the adjacent port was more difficult than they'd imagined, but once there it was a simple matter to conceal themselves from the guards and at the right moment jump aboard the cargo conveyer. Rick thought about mice and rats again as the team was carried out of Breetai's flagship and into the purple-armored cruiser.

Azonia was the commander of the cruiser and her all-female crew. Highly skilled, respected, and powerful, she had earned a reputation for succeeding where others had failed. Her attractiveness and magnetism had helped secure a brilliant career, but her soft eyes and small features belied the arrogant, self-absorbed megalomaniac many knew her to be. Here was one who would sacrifice half her fleet to fulfill that all-consuming passion for victory—a fact that had endeared her to the Zentraedi Command but one that instilled fear in the hearts of anyone of lesser station. In fact, among all the Zentraedi there was only one who would have defended her to the finish and whose respect for her some said was tainted by an atavistic lust for sensual experience. That one was Khyron, the so-called Backstabber.

Azonia was joined on the bridge of the cruiser by the ace pilot Dolza had promised her to carry out the infiltration—Miriya Parino of the Quadrono Battalion.

If Miriya was not as ambitious as her superior, she was certainly as respected. Where Azonia lived for self-glorification, Miriya fought for personal perfection: to rank first in this game called war the Zentraedi had been born into. Ever on the alert for new challenges, new tasks to master, new worlds to conquer, she was possessed of an intensely curious nature well suited to the extraordinary level of her talents, a trait that set her apart from the other pilots. But she was loyal to a fault and never failed to carry out her orders to the fullest. In this way she was much like her commander, but where Azonia would seek out ways to promote herself, only Miriya could rightfully judge Miriya. She had earned her own command a dozen times over but had rejected it on each occasion. Promotion would have placed her too far from the action, and it was hands-on action that she craved—contest, confrontation, challenge. She had little patience for the relative ease of a commander's life, having always to be ready to accept blame or praise based on how well the troops had carried out their mission. No, it was far easier to accept the orders of those unskilled superiors and bask in the freedom that a secondary position allowed.

She was eager to mix it up with these Micronians. They were making fools of the pilots under Breetai's command. And even the great Khyron had not fared well with this new enemy.

It was time to let the female Zentraedi take over.

Anyone unaware of the motivational differences between Azonia and Miriya might have been inclined to read rivalry into their relationship, and in fact many of the female soldiers on the bridge did just that, even though no such condition existed.

Azonia swirled the gray commander's cloak over her crimson uniform as she turned to face the female ace. Her close-cropped bluestone-colored hair gave her an air of efficiency. Unlike Miriya's long thick fall of forest green and large emerald eyes that radiated sensual fire.

"I take it you have already been briefed on your mission."

"I have, Commander Azonia. But may I speak freely?"

"Say what's on your mind."

"Delivering spies into the SDF-1 hardly seems a mission worthy of my talents."

"Yes, I thought it might be something like that."

"After all, I'm a combat pilot, not some delivery drone."

"This mission happens to be of utmost importance. It has been authorized by Commander-in-Chief Dolza himself."

"Of course, sir, but still—"

"Have you considered that these Micronians might prove to be more dangerous than you have been led to believe?"

"That is something to be hoped for, Commander."

"Need I remind you that my reputation rides on this mission?"

Miriya bowed and saluted. "I will not fail you, my lord."

Azonia narrowed her yes.

"The three micronized operatives are presently aboard our sister ship. They have been placed inside a capsule-craft that you will retrieve once we are within range of the dimensional fortress. Now, how will you get the spies aboard?"

"I am not at liberty to discuss that aspect of the operation with anyone."

The commander stiffened somewhat. "I see."

"Commander, it will be good to best Breetai in this matter. And Khyron, of course."

"*Commander* Khyron to you, Miriya—now and always. Is that clear?"

"My apologies, sir."

"You are dismissed. Return to your quarters and prepare for hyperspace-fold."

The fold operation was the first note of encouragement struck for the four Micronian escapees who had sequestered themselves in a supply hangar elsewhere in Azonia's cruiser. The Zentraedi guards had left the hold when the spacefold began, leaving them alone in a room full of armaments and Battlepods. But they remained cautiously optimistic. Especially Ben.

"I know a way we can pass the time—we can count the number of different places we might end up after this fold."

Lisa's attention had been riveted on the real-time indicator, but Ben's comment intruded on her concentration.

"Lieutenant Hunter, you didn't tell me you had such a comedian on your team." Lisa gestured to Ben. "We've gone from the frying pan to the fire, and all he can do is make jokes."

"All right Ben, can it," said Rick.

"How are we going to get outta here, anyway?" said Max. "Even if we do defold back in Earthspace?"

"We're going to commandeer one of these Battle-pods."

Lisa said it so matter-of-factly that the three men did delayed double takes.

"Just climb into the Battlepod and fly it out of here, huh? Who's going to teach us how to operate it? You think they left an operating manual inside, in the glove compartment maybe?"

Lisa put her hands on her hips. "Have you been playing hooky, Lieutenant?"

"Wait a minute!" Rick said defensively. "Sure, I've studied the insides of these things just like everybody else. But those were wrecks. Nobody's actually piloted one of them."

"Listen, Rick, you said yourself that their systems are complex but not impossible to understand. It shouldn't be a problem for three ace pilots like you boys."

"Come on, Commander..."

Lisa checked her watch. "It took us twenty-four real hours to make the hyperspace jump from Earthspace to Dolza's command center. Assuming we're headed back to the SDF-1, we've got twenty hours left to learn."

"And suppose we're not headed back to Earthspace? Suppose we defold at some other Zentraedi front or base or I don't know what?"

"Then it won't matter whether we learn how to operate it or not."

Rick stood up and cracked his knuckles. "All right, gang, let's get crackin'."

Aft in the special weapons hold, Miriya strapped herself into the Quadrono scout ship—a combination thruster unit and multiple-missile launcher developed by the Invid, and designed for infiltration or solo penetration operations.

Defold was complete, and the time had come to retrieve the three micronized agents from the cruiser's sister ship.

Miriya lowered the canopy of the extravehicular pack and stepped forward to the edge of the port. In the distance she could see the object of her mission: the SDF-1. It was under attack by the remnants of Breetai's tattered fleet.

Azonia came on-screen in the mecha's cockpit:

"We'll draw the enemy's attention away from you. May you win all your battles!"

"As always!"

Miriya launched herself into space, a darting dragon-fly among the stars . . .

Max had his arms stretched out deep into the pod's waldolike gun controls. Ben was scratching his head, puzzling over the firing mechanism for the missiles. Lisa wondered how she was going to be able to activate those huge radio toggles. And Rick tried to figure out how he was going to fly the thing.

The interior of the Battlepod was not entirely dissimilar to human-made Robotech mecha. In fact, the design of the cockpit went a long way toward verifying Lisa's theory about a point of common origin; the layout and placement of the controls had the logic of human construction, albeit on a grand scale.

Lisa, her arms overhead hugging a toggle switch, glanced at her watch and dropped to the sphere's seat. She looked hard at her companions, calculating the present level of visual distortion against the indicator's display. Satisfied with the results of her scan, she announced:

"We're coming out of defold right on schedule. It's got to be Earthspace or an incredible coincidence."

The four regarded one another and took a collective breath; they all knew what had to be done next.

Rick readied himself at the controls. "Let's see if we can start this thing up."

He engaged the drive lever and activated the sensor and scanner systems. The mecha began to hum and come to life, and the first thing that greeted their eyes on the forward screen was the sight of two Zentraedi soldiers just returned to the hanger.

The soldiers spun around at the sound of the activated pod.

"They're on to us!" yelled Rick.

"Blast 'em!"

Max shouted, "Here goes nothing!" as laser bolts shot from the arm cannons and dropped the guards to the deck.

Lisa and Ben cheered. Rick told Max to keep firing.

"Keep it up; let's open up this can of worms and get out of here." Meanwhile, he nudged the stick forward and the Battlepod lifted away from its still silent companions.

Max continued to pour particle heat into the hull, until all at once the lasers burned through, and air and mecha were being sucked in a rush toward the breach.

"We're gonna have to be fast," Max warned them. "These things heal themselves."

Ben said, "Not while I'm around!" and loosed two rockets at the hull.

Rick let out a rousing yell. Simultaneously with the explosions, he sent the thruster stick home; the pod soared across the hangar and through the breach.

Miriya had retrieved the ejected canister which contained the micronized agents. Battlepods were swarming around Zor's ship like angry insects and engaging enemy mecha throughout the field. It would have been a simple matter to insert the cannister and be done with it, but she couldn't resist testing these waters.

She flew straight into their midst, executing a series of teasing maneuvers meant to draw the enemy out; but not one of them succeeded in getting a fix on her. She made up her mind that these Micronians were nothing to worry about and grew even more daring, positioning herself in the center of an entire squadron of enemy fighters. And again their heat-seekers could not find the mark. She laughed aloud and stung back.

Roy Fokker, Skull Team leader, would later recall the strange sight he witnessed that day: how a Zentraedi mecha, not much larger than a giant with a jet pack, had taken out five VTs at once.

Through the breach, the commandeered Battlepod rolled into a near front gainer and was almost taken out by Zentraedi crossfire. But the occupants of that pod were filled with such vigor and élan that they scarcely took notice of their predicament. Ahead of them, enveloped in a cloud of metal anger, was their ship. And beyond that, their planet and its silver satellite.

"Can you raise anything on the radio?"

"I'm trying," said Lisa. Ben came to her aid; together they put their strength to the knob and managed to give it a fraction of a turn.

Rick heard singing: a familiar voice, a familiar song.

"That's Minmei! That's her song—'My Boyfriend's a Pilot'!"

"As long as it's not *was* a pilot," said Ben.

Miriya easily avoided the Phalanx and Valkyrie fire from the SDF-1 and came alongside the fortress at a point where Breetai claimed the hull could be easily breached. She summoned Protoculture strength to the outsize grappler hands of the mecha and tore away some new hatchway the Micronians had installed. She deposited the cylinder inside an air lock in the mecha, then opened and resealed.

"Insertion successful," Miriya said aloud. "Returning to base."

Status reports, enemy trajectories, battle coordinates...

"We've got the military frequency," said Rick excitedly.

Lisa leaned into the mike. "Please respond, SDF-1, we are in your air space. This is Commander Hayes and the Vermilion Team attempting to make contact with our home base. Do you read me? Over. Rick, do you think they heard us?"

"I hope so, Lisa. I'd hate to be taken out by one of our own VTs."

Three Battloids were closing on the pod in attack formation, gatling cannons in hand. Rick and Lisa, Ben and Max, turned to each other with undisguised looks of concern.

"Did they hear us, Rick? Did they hear us?!"

Rick closed his eyes as the Battloids moved in for the kill.

With home so close you could almost touch it...

The following chapter is a sneak preview of *Homecoming* —Book III in the continuing saga of ROBOTECH!!

CHAPTER
ONE

*The enemy armada, so vastly superior to us in numbers
of fighting mecha and aggregate firepower, continues to
harry and harass us. But time and again the Zentraedi stop
short of all-out attack. They impede our long voyage back to
Earth, but they cannot stop us. I am still uncertain as to
what good fortune is working in the SDF-1's favor.*

*I do not point out any of this to the crew or refugees,
however. It does no good to tell grieving friends and loved
ones that casualties could have been far worse.*

From the log of Captain Henry Gloval

BLUE LINES OF ENEMY CANNON FIRE STREAKED BY
Roy Fokker's cockpit, scorching one of his Veritech
fighter's tail stabilizers, ranging in for a final volley.

"Flying sense" the aviators called it, jargon that came
from the twentieth century term "air sense": honed and
superior high-speed piloting instincts. It was something a
raw beginner took a while to develop, something that
separated the novices from the vets.

And it was something Lieutenant Commander Roy
Fokker, Skull Team leader and Veritech squadron commander, had in abundance, even in the airlessness of a
deep-space dogfight.

Responding to his deft touch at the controls and his very will—passed along to it by Robotech sensors in his flight helmet—Roy's Veritech fighter did a wingover and veered onto a new vector with tooth-snapping force. Thrusters blaring full-bore, the maneuver forces pressed him into his seat, just as the enemy was concentrating more on his aim than on his flying.

The Zentraedi in the Battlepod on Roy's tail, trying so diligently to kill him and destroy his Robotech fighter, was a good pilot, steady and cool like all of them, but he lacked Roy's flying abilities.

While the giant alien gaped, astounded, at his suddenly empty gunsight reticle, the Skull Team leader was already coming around behind the pod into the kill position.

Around that fragment of the battle, an enormous dogfight raged as Zentraedi pods and their Cyclops recon ships mixed it up ferociously with the grimly determined human defenders in their Veritechs. The bright spherical explosions characteristic of zero-g battle blossomed all around, dozens at a time. Blue Zentraedi radiation blasts were matched by the Veritechs' autocannons, which flung torrents of high-density armorpiercers at the enemy.

Roy was relieved to see that the SDF-1 was unharmed. Most of the fighting seemed to be going on at some distance from it, although it was clear that the enemy fleet had all the odds on its side. The Zentraedi armada easily numbered over a million warships.

Roy located his wingman, Captain Kramer, in the furious engagement; forming up for mutual security, he looked around again for the fantastic Zentraedi mecha that had done so much damage a few minutes before. It had flown rings around the Veritechs that had gone after it, taking Roy and the Skulls by surprise and smashing their formation after cutting a swath through Vermilion Team.

Whatever it was, it was unlike any Zentraedi weapon the humans had seen so far. Unlike the pods, which resembled towering metal ostriches bristling with guns, the newcomer was more human shaped—a bigger, more hulking and heavily armed and armored version of the Veritechs' own Battloid mode. And fast—frightfully fast and impossible to stop, eluding even the SDF-1's massive defensive barrages.

Roy had expected to see the battle fortress under intense attack; instead, the super dimensional fortress was cruising along unbothered and alone. Moreover, transmissions over the tac net indicated that the Zentraedi pods and Cyclopes were withdrawing. Roy couldn't figure that out.

He switched from the tac net to SDF-1's command net. There was word of the new Zentraedi mecha. The thing had made it as far as SDF-1—getting in beneath the fields of fire of most of the ship's batteries—then had suddenly withdrawn at blinding speed, outmaneuvering gunfire and outracing pursuit. The ship had suffered only minor damage, and the operations and intelligence people had concluded that the whole thing had been a probing attack of some kind, a test of a new machine and new tactics.

Roy didn't care as long as the battle fortress was still safe. He gathered the Veritechs, ready to head home.

"Enemy pod," Skull Five called over the tac net. "Bearing one-niner-four-seven."

Roy already had the computer reference on one of his situation screens. A pod, all right, but evidently damaged and drifting, none of its weapons firing; it was leaking atmosphere.

"Could be a trick," Skull Seven said. "What d' ya think, skipper? Do we blast it out of the sky?"

"Negative; somebody may still be alive in there, and a

live captive is what the intelligence staff's been praying for." The incredible savagery of this deep-space war was such that few survived as casualties. Alien or human, a fighter almost always either triumphed or died, a simple formula. The humans had never recovered a living enemy.

Besides, for very personal reasons, Roy was especially eager to see a Zentraedi undergo interrogation.

"We're getting signals from it, nothing we can unscramble," a communications officer reported over the command net.

Whatever was going on, none of the Zentraedi forces seemed to be turning back for a rescue. Veritech fly-bys drew no fire; eyeball inspection and instruments indicated that the damaged pod's main power source had been knocked out but that some of its weapons were still functioning. Nevertheless, it passed up several opportunities to blast away at nearby VTs.

"This is too good an opportunity to pass up," Gloval finally announced over the main command net. "If there is a survivor aboard, we must get him into the SDF-1 immediately."

"That thing could be booby-trapped—or its occupant could be!" a security staff officer protested from one of Roy's display screens.

Gloval replied, "That is why we will push the pod closer to SDF-1—but not too close—and connect a boarding tube to it. An EVA team will make a thorough examination before we permit it any closer."

"But—" the officer began.

Roy cut in over the command net, "You heard the captain, so put a sock in it, mac!" Roy was elated with Gloval's decision; it was only a slim hope, but now there *was* hope of finding out what had happened to Roy's closest friend in the world, Rick Hunter and Lisa Hayes and the others who'd disappeared on their desperate mission to guide the SDF-1 through danger.

Roy began swinging into place, shifting his ship to Battloid mode. "Okay, Skull Team; time to play a little bumper cars."

Two more Skulls went to Battloid, their Robotech ships transforming and reconfiguring. When the shift was complete, the war machines looked like enormous armored ultramech knights.

They joined Roy in pushing the inert pod back toward the battle fortress.

The men and women of the EVA—Extravehicular Activity—crews were efficient and careful. *They're also gutsy as hell*, Roy reflected, his Battloid towering over them in the boarding tube lock. But of course, everybody knew and honored the legendary dedication and tenacity of the EVA crews.

Crowded into the boarding tube lock with two other Battloids behind him, Roy watched expectantly. The huge lock, extending from the SDF-1 at the end of nearly a mile of large-diameter tube, was a yawning dome on a heavy base, equipped with every sort of contingency gear imaginable. The captured pod and EVA crew and Roy's security detail took up only a small part of its floor space.

"Not beat up too bad," the EVA crew chief observed over the com net. "But I dunno how much air it lost. What d' ya say, Fokker? Do we open 'er up?" She was holding a thermotorch ready. She'd turned to gaze up at Roy's cockpit.

As ranking officer on the scene, Lt. Comdr. Roy Fokker had the responsibility of advising Gloval. Tampering with the pod was very risky; they could trigger some kind of booby trap humans couldn't even imagine, destroying everyone there and perhaps even damaging the SDF-1.

But we can't go on fighting the war this way! Roy thought. *Knowing next to nothing about these creatures we're up against or even why we're fighting—we can't go on like this much longer!*

"Cap'n Gloval, sir, I say we take a shot."

"Very well. Good luck to you," Gloval answered. "Proceed."

Roy reached down and put a giant hand in front of the EVA crew chief, blocking her way as she approached the enemy mecha. "Sorry, Pietra; this is my party."

His Battloid stood upright again and walked to the pod, shouldering its autocannon, its footsteps shaking the deck. "Cover me," he told his teammates, and they fanned out, muzzles leveled for clear fields of fire. The Battloid's forearms extruded metal tentacles, complicated waldos and manipulators, and thermotorches.

"Just try not to break anything unnecessarily," Pietra warned, and led her crew to the shelter of a blast shield.

Roy looked the pod over, trying a few external controls tentatively. Nothing happened. He moved closer still, examining the pressure seals that ran around the great hatch at the rear top of the pod's bulbous torso. Being this close to a pod's guns had him sweating under his VT helmet.

"Careful, Roy," Kramer said quietly.

He didn't want to use the torch for fear of fire or explosion. He decided to try simply pulling the pod's hatch open with the Battloid's huge strong hands. He ran his ship's fingers along the seams, feeling for a place to grab hold . . .

The pod shook, rattled, and began to open.

ABOUT THE AUTHOR

Jack McKinney has been a psychiatric aide, fusion-rock guitarist and session man, worldwide wilderness guide, and "consultant" to the U.S. Military in Southeast Asia (although they had to draft him for that).

His numerous other works of mainstream and science fiction—novels, radio and television scripts—have been written under various pseudonyms.

He currently resides in Dos Lagunas, El Petén, Guatemala.

ROBOTECH ™

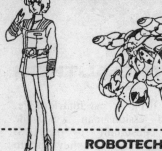

ROBOTECH COMICS ARE TOTALLY AWESOME!!!

Subscribe now and get in on all the excitement of today's hottest comic book series . . . ROBOTECH from Comico The Comic Company! Each month, a new 32-page, four-color comic will be delivered to your home.

**Send today to: ROBOTECH COMICS
1547 DeKALB STREET
NORRISTOWN, PA 19401**

☐ **ROBOTECH Macross Saga** $9.00
Thrill to the adventure and romance of Lt. Rick Hunter and Lynn Minmei as they battle the evil Breetai and his Zentraedi warriors.

☐ **ROBOTECH Masters** $9.00
Cheer on Lt. Dana Sterling and her 15th Squadron as Zor and hordes of alien bioroids attack the earth.

☐ **ROBOTECH The New Generation** $9.00
Scott Bernard commandeers the fiercest group of freedom fighters the earth has ever seen. His mission—to get to Reflex Point, no matter what the cost!

Or, you can get the story that started it all!!!

☐ **ROBOTECH The Graphic Novel** $5.95
This is it! Genesis: Robotech. The origin story of the entire Robotech saga featuring Roy Fokker and Rick Hunter. Understand the mysteries of protoculture in this beautifully illustrated, full-color, 48-page graphic novel.

Please send me the Comico comics I have checked above. I am enclosing $_____.

NAME_____AGE_____

STREET_____

CITY_____STATE_____ZIP_____

Sorry, no back issues! Your subscription begins with the next available issue. Make check or money order payable to Comico The Comic Company. No cash or C.O.D.'s please. Price includes shipping and handling. Please allow 10-12 weeks for delivery of your first issue. Canadian orders, send U.S. currency only.

COMICO THE COMIC COMPANY
© 1987 Harmony Gold U.S.A., Inc./Tatsunoko Production Company, Ltd.
"ROBOTECH" is a trademark owned and licensed by Revell, Inc. Used here with permission.